GAY

Please return / renew by date shown.
You can renew it at:
norlink.norfolk.gov.uk
or by telephone: 0344 800 8006
Please have your library card & PIN ready

PS

CL

05 NOV

12 MAR 14

09. APR 14

02. 14.

23. DEC 14

22. JAN

NORFOLK LIBRARY
AND INFORMATION SERVICE

D0233811

MYSTERY DATE

BY
CRYSTAL GREEN

All the characters in this book have no existence outside the imagination of the author, and have no relation whatsoever to anyone bearing the same name or names. They are not even distantly inspired by any individual known or unknown to the author, and all the incidents are pure invention.

All Rights Reserved including the right of reproduction in whole or in part in any form. This edition is published by arrangement with Harlequin Enterprises II B.V./S.à.r.l. The text of this publication or any part thereof may not be reproduced or transmitted in any form or by any means, electronic or mechanical, including photocopying, recording, storage in an information retrieval system, or otherwise, without the written permission of the publisher.

This book is sold subject to the condition that it shall not, by way of trade or otherwise, be lent, resold, hired out or otherwise circulated without the prior consent of the publisher in any form of binding or cover other than that in which it is published and without a similar condition including this condition being imposed on the subsequent purchaser.

® and ™ are trademarks owned and used by the trademark owner and/or its licensee. Trademarks marked with ® are registered with the United Kingdom Patent Office and/or the Office for Harmonisation in the Internal Market and in other countries.

First published in Great Britain 2013
by Mills & Boon, an imprint of Harlequin (UK) Limited,
Eton House, 18-24 Paradise Road, Richmond, Surrey TW9 1SR

© Chris Marie Green 2013

ISBN: 978 0 263 90516 8

30-0913

Harlequin (UK) policy is to use papers that are natural, renewable and recyclable products and made from wood grown in sustainable forests. The logging and manufacturing processes conform to the legal environmental regulations of the country of origin.

Printed and bound in Spain
by Blackprint CPI, Barcelona

Crystal Green lives near Las Vegas, where she writes for the Mills & Boon® Cherish™ and Blaze® lines. She loves to read, overanalyze movies and TV programs, practice yoga and travel when she can. You can read more about her at www.crystal-green.com, where she has a blog and contests. Also, you can follow her on Twitter, @CrystalGreenMe.

1

LEIGH VAUGHN SAT in a car with one of her best friends, staring at the imposing beach-cliff house where her mystery date was supposed to take place tonight.

As she kept staring, she swallowed. Hard.

Margot spoke from the driver's seat. "'Last night I dreamt I went to Manderley again.'"

Leigh pulled her gaze away from the house. "What?"

"That's the first line from *Rebecca*." Margot raised a well-manicured brow, turning her light green-blue gaze to Leigh. Her high cheekbones and tousled, layered dark hair gave her a look that fell somewhere between a pixie and a wild child, but her designer knit dress was all high-class. "Don't you get a certain vibe from this place, just like the narrator in that book did after she found out her new husband's first wife, Rebecca, pretty much haunted Manderley?"

Leigh wished she hadn't brought Miss Cal-U English Major with her. Better yet, she just wished that Margot would lay off teasing her about tonight. Some moral support would be nice right about now.

"It's only a date," Leigh said, echoing the words that

had been going through her head all day. She wasn't sure if she was just trying to shut Margot up or calm herself down.

"A date," Margot said, a sparkle in her gaze. "In a huge Gothic house. And with a man who won't tell you who he is."

"Why don't you make this sound even more intimidating, Marg? Because I'm not nervous enough."

"Maybe you should be very nervous." Margot gave an "ooo, how scary" look to the mansion that loomed above them at the end of the gated driveway under the dusk-burnished November sky. "When Mystery Man bought your basket at the charity auction, I didn't think you'd actually go through with this. But you've surprised me, Leigh. Maybe you've got a little adventure in you, after all."

Adventure.

Good God—that was what she'd come here for, wasn't it?

She followed Margot's gaze toward that gray stone mansion again, with its imposing balconies and arches. The man who was waiting for Leigh in there had spent $5,000 to win her basket about a month ago during a reunion for her college sorority, Tau Epsilon Gamma, and its counterpart, the agricultural business–centered fraternity Phi Rho Mu.

Leigh took in a deep breath. Even back in college, smack in the middle of the rural San Joaquin Valley, she'd never done something this crazy—not during pledging, not during all their parties…never. True, she, Margot and their friend Dani had been good-time girls, best friends enjoying their youth, but that was when the silliness was supposed to end—after they graduated and became adults.

But no. She and Margot just *had* to go and put on that auction at the ten-year reunion. They'd just had to hold out for the highest bids on all those baskets that contained materials for a date with the women who'd created them. Margot had called her basket Around the Girl in Eighty Ways, and after her spicy encounters with the man who'd purchased the basket—her archenemy from college, of all people—she'd ended up getting engaged to him.

Leigh had taken a sweeter route. She'd stayed true to the wholesome country-girl Tau image and named her basket "A Taste of Honey"; she'd intended to give whoever won it a down-home dinner laced with the main ingredient—and maybe more, depending who bought the basket.

But she hadn't expected what happened next—a fellow sorority sister, Beth Dahrling, had been the highest bidder, and she'd revealed that she was acting as a liaison for a man who refused to disclose his identity.

Leigh would've never guessed that she was eventually going to end up in front of a mansion that belonged in some kind of "It was a dark and stormy night" book.

She slid down in her seat. "I can't believe you got me into this, Marg."

"Me? How?"

As Margot waited for an answer, Leigh realized that she'd been plucking at the seam of her jeans, and she stopped. Her date had requested that she "dress casual," just as she did on the country-cooking show she hosted on the Food Network—denim, boots, yee-haw blouses and all.

And what the hell? She'd gone along with it. But now her lacy flowered blouse seemed to show too much cleavage, and her jeans clung too tightly, reminding her of what she'd felt like over a year ago when she'd still been packing extra pounds.

Margot chuffed. "You're not squirming out of an answer to this one, Leigh. How is it my fault that you ended up in this situation? You're the one who said yes to the conditions after Beth bought the basket."

Right or wrong, she was so on edge that she said the first thing that came to mind. "You're the one who made up the baskets in the first place. When we heard that Dani was going to give up on her big wedding plans, you thought of the date auction to help her raise money for her extravaganza."

"Not that it did much good since Dani refused the money and decided to go small." Margot lasered a knowing look at her. "You're only ticked off because I made my basket as sexy as hell, and you didn't want to be outdone. Say it—I'm totally right, aren't I?"

Leigh shot her an irritated glance, but it wasn't exactly all about Margot. She was merely stalling by sitting here saying dumb stuff and creating an argument.

But she wasn't sure just why she was so reluctant to get out of the car. There'd been a restless growl rolling through her ever since she had heard about Margot's hot basket and what Leigh could put in hers, too. Hell, if she were telling the whole truth, she would even have to admit that the growl had started about a year ago, when she'd dropped the weight she'd carried since she was a kid.

The growl made her stay up most nights, running her hand over her belly, circling, then going lower, trying to give herself what she'd never gotten from all the ho-hum sex she'd had before with the lights off so that her few, steady partners wouldn't see all her bulges and cellulite.

And so that they wouldn't call her "Cushions," just as they had in college when she'd been pledging with Margot and Dani.

"Sorry," Leigh finally said, absently toying with the seam on her jeans again. "I'm pretty nervous, and I'm saying things I don't mean."

Margot softened. "Are you sure it's not excitement you're feeling?"

That could've been it, too. "There're just a bunch of second thoughts attacking me right now. I keep thinking that if you hadn't been so adventurous with your basket, I probably wouldn't have been so daring with mine. Dumb, dumb, dumb. Why didn't I just offer an innocent little picnic at the reunion and leave it at that?"

Margot bit her lip, and Leigh could tell she was stifling a laugh. They'd always been competitive—when they were dorm roommates, when they'd lived together at the sorority house, even after college when Margot, the Girl Most Likely to Succeed, had shot to infamy with all the "single woman on the go" travel books she'd written. Margot had always made Leigh want to be better, to keep up with her, and the baskets had been no exception.

"I suppose you're right," Margot said. "This *is* all my fault. I'm an awful person for making you want to have some fun."

A moment passed; then they both laughed and for a moment Leigh's nerves actually mellowed.

But the sight of the mansion on the hill remained in her peripheral vision, and she didn't laugh for long.

Seriously—what *was* she getting herself into?

That familiar growl gnawed through her belly, making her ache a little between her legs. *Admit it,* she thought. *You want this.*

She wanted to let go of all her chubby-girl neuroses, wanted to see what it would be like to come out of her modest closet in a big way. She wanted to go on a mystery date with her own sexy basket and the taste of honey it offered, literally with a humdinger of a meal, and figuratively with…

Oh, God, she had no idea what else was in store for her tonight.

Margot got out her smartphone, dialing it as she glanced at Leigh. "You need an extra push out of this car, sweetie." Then she smiled brightly. "Dani? I'm putting you on speakerphone with me and Leigh."

Dani, who rounded out their best-friend group, was laughing when she came on the line. Leigh could almost imagine her, with her curly bobbed red hair, her doe-gray eyes and her milk-pale skin. She tried *not* to think about the look on Dani's face that she caught sometimes…. Was it disappointment that she wouldn't have the grand nuptials she'd always dreamed of, ever since college when they'd nicknamed her "Hearts"? Or was it the cold feet Leigh and Margot suspected Dani might be suffering after an engagement that had lasted for years now?

"You haven't gone into his place yet?" Dani asked Leigh.

Leigh rolled her eyes. "Aren't you supposed to be catering for someone?"

"I'm on a break at work, just like I was when I gave you a pep talk before you left the hotel. I wish I could've driven down there with Margot to meet you."

Leigh shot the phone a disgruntled glance as Margot laughed and said, "You've got work, and *I've* got this covered, Dan. Except I wish you were here to help me kick Leigh's butt up this long driveway. You should see what's at the end of it. The mansion is straight out of *Jane Eyre* or—"

Leigh cut her off. "Margot is having a grand old time, Dani. She's playing on my last nerve because it's hilarious to her."

Margot shrugged innocently. "You're so easy to mess with, though."

"Just don't listen to Margot," Dani said. "It's not like you're going into an unsafe place, Leigh. Beth Dahrling said she'd meet you there, right?"

Beth Dahrling, the woman who'd bid on Leigh's basket in place of the Mystery Man.

"Right," Leigh said. "But I doubt she'll be chaperoning the whole night. She's just a friend of this guy, and she set everything up."

"She's a fellow sister. Plus, she told you that Mystery Man was a brother in our very favorite fraternity, and a brother would never put you in a bad situation."

True. Riley, Dani's fiancé and a Phi Rho Mu brother to boot, had all but promised Leigh that one of his own would never harm her. Besides, Beth would be here. Still, Riley had no idea of Mystery Man's identity, although he'd done enough online research to try and uncover it. Margot put a hand on Leigh's arm, and it was a comforting touch. "It'll be a good time, you'll see. My bet is that he's just one of the fraternity brothers— a San Joaquin cowboy whose ranch is making the big bucks—and he's having some fun with you. He'll ask the TV chef to cook him dinner, and while you're eating, you'll have a major laugh over this whole secrecy thing."

Leigh locked gazes with Margot, her frenemy, the woman who'd always had everything come so easily to her. The person Leigh had wanted to emulate in college and beyond, even as they went toe-to-toe with each other.

It was as if Margot saw all of that in Leigh's eyes, and for some reason she glanced away.

This wasn't the first time Margot had acted like this recently, and Leigh had been wondering why. Her friend had started a new book about a city girl living the country life on Clint's cutting-horse ranch, and she had a new blog that was drawing all kinds of interest. So why did she occasionally look as if she was hiding something?

Leigh wanted to ask what was going on, but Dani was already speaking on the phone.

"Well?" she asked. "Are you going to stay in that car all night or are you going to have an adventure?"

Leigh sent one last look to the mansion, her stomach in knots…

And that growl combing over every inch of her.

ADAM MORGAN LEANED against the wall near a barred window in the top story of the rented house. He was watching the Prius that was parked at the end of the long driveway, near the open iron gates that separated him from the eucalyptus-shrouded lane that led up here.

"She's not coming in, is she?" he asked.

Next to him, his good friend Beth Dahrling was also peering out the window. "Well, Leigh's here, at least. I don't think she would come this far to turn around."

She had to be right, because he had hired a small

plane, in cash, to fly Leigh down here to the Pismo Beach area from her home up in Lodi. He'd decided to have this dinner away from Avila Grande, where they'd both attended Cal-U.

For a short time, in Adam's case.

He glanced over his shoulder at Beth, whose long dark hair was swept back into a tortoiseshell barrette. In her chic printed silk wrap dress and with her rosy-brown skin, she seemed colorful and exotic, but the melancholy expression she wore gave him pause.

"You still think this is a bad idea," he said, a trace of amusement in his voice.

"I think it's an odd one." She turned her liquid-brown gaze on him. "I think all you had to do was bid on Leigh's basket and reveal who you were."

"She wouldn't remember me." He hadn't stuck around the university long enough for there to even be a picture of him on the walls of the fraternity house, where he'd pledged for only a short time before he'd had to drop out and return home.

But several months ago, when he'd seen Leigh on TV for the first time, he'd certainly remembered *her*. And when Beth had mentioned the basket auction that was being held at the reunion for their connected organizations, he'd thought of Leigh as she had been fourteen years ago, laughing all the time, taking a moment to smile at the shy freshman pledge who didn't say much to girls—the kid who'd disappeared without ever becoming an official Phi Rho Mu brother.

Beth sighed and walked away from the window. Adam turned around, folding his arms over his chest while she spoke.

"Do you blame her for being cautious about this?"

she asked. "For all she knows, you could be the Phantom of the Opera in this old house."

He dodged her comment. "I didn't want to use any of my own homes." Not for a one-night basket date that had sparked his imagination.

"You know damned well that it's not your homes I'm talking about," Beth said. "Really, Adam, this is the strangest thing you've ever done. In fact…"

She didn't have to say anything else. Ever since his wife, Carla, had withered away from breast cancer two years ago, he had become a recluse, uninterested in most things that happened outside the walls of his homes, except for the many property and business investments that he'd inherited from Carla, money that kept his bank accounts flush, thanks to the way he'd multiplied the investments.

"Hey," he said, walking over to Beth and reaching out, chucking her under the chin with his finger. "This is going to turn out all right. No worries."

Beth rolled her eyes. "Yes, it'll turn out all right for you. This date will provide some temporary entertainment, and then you'll move on to whatever comes next. I've seen it before with your women, but none of them have ever been one of my sisters."

She was talking about the women he'd met online. Women he would talk to behind yet another wall—this one created by the computer. They provided mental fantasies for him, and that was all he'd needed for a couple of years now.…

Until he'd seen Leigh on TV, wearing a red-and-white-checkered shirt that was unbuttoned down to *here*, her stomach bared because of the knot she'd tied above her waist, her long blond hair pinned away from her heart-shaped face and tumbling down her back as she worked in her *Come-on Down Kitchen* by candlelight, creating sensual country meals on her show.

She'd taken off a lot of weight since college, but he thought she'd looked just as beautiful with her curves and soft skin back then. He'd first seen her at a casual party populated mostly by his fraternity brothers and the Tau Epsilon Gamma sorority, and his heart had skipped a beat while she'd joked with her friends across the room. Her laugh had captured him in some physical way that he'd never been able to explain, but it had consumed him that night, and he'd never forgotten. And that smile she'd given him in passing—that dazzling, pure smile that had reached inside and grabbed him…. If he'd been less shy, he would've taken that as encouragement, but the fact that he'd never had the chance made Leigh Vaughn into a figment of his college imagination, made her into the ultimate "what could've been" girl.

Of course, that had been just before he was called home after his dad succumbed to a heart attack and Adam had taken up the mantle of "man of the house."

He turned back around, moving to the window again. He could see that the car was still parked, and even now his heart flipped. But it wasn't because of some old never-consummated crush. It was because of tonight's scenario.

The basket.

He'd initiated all of this out of sheer curiosity. How had Leigh turned out so many years later? Did she still have the same warmth a man could feel even from across a room?

Adam gripped the window frame. He wasn't someone who needed warmth—it was the curiosity that was driving him. That was all. And these days he could afford to appease it.

He could afford almost anything that broke up the boredom.

As he kept looking through the barred window, he could faintly see his reflection: dark hair and nearly gold eyes from his mom's Spanish heritage, a mouth drawn tight. A man wearing a black shirt and jeans. Someone he barely recognized.

"This is only a harmless date, Beth," he said. "For everyone involved."

"I'll bet Leigh's ready to jump out of her skin. Does that turn you on or something?"

He paused. Did it turn him on to know that she was wondering who he was?

Yeah. Yeah, it did. And he liked that she would never know enough about him to contact him for another date if she got it in her head that she wanted more. He didn't do attachments. Not anymore, not after Carla had taken his heart with her.

Beth walked away, her footsteps thudding on the polished wood floor.

"I'm going out there," she said.

"To drag her inside?"

"I don't know what I'll do, but this is ridiculous. Almost as ridiculous as being the executive assistant to a man who wants to stay in the shadows during his entire date."

He laughed. His plan for dinner did sound demented. But he was in the mood for it. Besides, how was keeping a distance from his date any different from getting to know all those women online? There he could be anyone, just like tonight.

No attachments, no strings. This was the ultimate safe date…and a game, if he had to admit it. And the more he thought about tonight's game, the more turned on he got.

Beth left the room, and Adam found himself holding his breath. He let it out, shaking his head. Carla would've thought he was going off-balance, too. She would've put her hands on her hips, asking him what the hell had happened to make him this way.

But Carla had always gotten straight to the point, even fourteen years ago after he'd returned to his family ranch, mourning his father, keeping his mother from shriveling into a depressed heap while helping her to run their cattle operation and raise his three younger siblings the best he could. Carla, seven years older and wiser, with a family so rich that they had already bequeathed her the gentleman's ranch next door, had come calling the second day after he'd settled in.

Yes, even back then Carla had offered a neighborly hand to the eighteen-year-old who was so out of his depth that he could barely catch four hours of sleep per night. And as the years went by, friendship had turned into love, then into a happy marriage.

Then she was gone.

Through the window, Beth appeared on the driveway, her skirt swishing around her legs as she strode down to the open gate and the car beyond it.

Adam held his breath yet again, watching to see if Leigh was going to get out of that car and embark on this strange date.

Or if she was going to leave, just as everyone in his life seemed to do.

"OH MY GOD, here she comes," Leigh said, sliding down in her car seat as she spied Beth walking down the driveway with purpose.

"Should we hide?"

The glee in Margot's tone told Leigh that her friend was teasing her again. Too bad Dani had already gotten off the phone, because she could've joined in the chiding.

Beth reached the iron gate, then waved, and Margot obviously couldn't resist one last gibe.

""Will you walk into my parlor?" said the Spider to the Fly.'"

The joke was the last straw for Leigh, and with one defiant glance at Margot, she sucked it up, opened the door and got out of the damned car.

The salt-tinged coastal wind threaded through her hair as she shut the door and put on a smile for Beth as they hugged in greeting.

Margot had gotten out, too, and she embraced Beth, then held her at arm's length.

"I always did admire your clothes," Margot said, surveying Beth's sleek multihued silk dress and her strappy gold sandals.

Beth smiled. "Even though you were a couple years behind me in college, I have to say that I looked up to your sense of style, too." She turned to Leigh. "So what do you think?"

About fashion? Global politics? The Kardashians? Or about the blindest date ever?

Margot saved her from having to answer. "Sorry about the delay. Dani called about some wedding plans, and we were just going over them with her in the car."

"Ah, yes. I hear Dani and Riley are having their ceremony on Clint's ranch." Beth laughed. "I mean, *your* ranch, Margot, now that you're living together."

Margot shrugged and actually blushed. Yeah, Margot, former queen of singletons, newly crowned empress of blushing.

"You heard right," she said. "We're hosting the wedding, and you'll be invited."

Then, as if she were a mom dropping off a child who didn't want to attend a birthday party with evil clowns, Margot scooted around to her side of the car.

"And that's my cue to scram." She winked at Leigh. "Have fun, you."

Beth took Leigh's arm to lead her up to the open gates, and Margot used her hand as a fake telephone, putting it up to her ear and mouthing, *Call me when you're done!*

Leigh widened her eyes at her friend, then turned around to walk with Beth up the driveway. Margot's car motor revved, then faded as she drove away.

And that was when it became official. This was happening. Mystery date with Mystery Man.

Beth squeezed Leigh's arm. "So Margot drove you over here?"

"She met me at the Sea Breeze Suites for a girls' weekend, so yeah. I didn't need the limo you offered."

"That doesn't really answer my question."

Shoot. "You're asking if she drove me here because I was cautious about this date?"

"Exactly." Beth laughed. "But that's smart, really, to bring along a friend. You can trust me, though."

"I do trust you." But the farther they got up the driveway, the more her stomach spun. And the more her body sang with an odd, almost warped thrill.

Her, Leigh Vaughn. She'd never, ever done anything like this before, and she was liking it. *A lot*.

Beth was clearly trying to put her at ease. "Your date got you everything you requested for dinner, from the ingredients to the cookware."

All the auction basket had promised was a meal featuring honey. Like Margot, Leigh had been careful in phrasing the notes in her basket, making sure that if she didn't want the date to go too far, she wouldn't have to live up to any wickedly spelled-out promises. But if she liked what she saw in Mystery Man and she wanted to go beyond food and give him a real taste of honey…

Every inch of her pulsated.

"How do you know him?" Leigh asked as they got to the top of the driveway, where gnarled bushes lined the lawn and the wind whistled a soft, meandering tune.

Beth had probably been expecting this question, and she launched right into an answer.

"I'm friends with him but also professional associates. Out of pure happenstance, he found my résumé online after college, and now he pays me nicely to take care of his business affairs."

"Didn't you get a law degree?"

"Yes, but there are a lot of legal angles to what I do for him. Contracts, boring stuff like that."

"And who exactly is 'him'?"

Beth laughed again. "Good try, but that's all you're going to get out of me."

As they arrived at the massive carved wood door, Leigh paused.

"Why is he taking such pains to be a mystery?" she asked, hoping that Beth would at least answer this.

Beth's smile straightened out as she hesitated, then

said, "Your basket was a game, Leigh, and he's making a countermove, continuing the game. It's all in fun."

A game? What kind of man played this way? And what sort of guy could afford a place like this?

She ran her gaze over that door, noticing the iron lion's-head knocker. "He's rich. I can tell that much."

"He's got a few bucks to spare. Did you run this address through the internet?"

Leigh nodded. The house was owned by a rental property that had led her and her friends to dead ends. "We assumed the place isn't his."

"It isn't. He's only vacationing." Beth reached out to open the door, but she hesitated again.

Meanwhile, all Leigh could hear was the sound of her heart *boom-boom-booming* through her.

Beth spoke, her hand still in midair. "It'll be a harmless, fun night," she repeated. "If you go inside with that in mind, you'll walk away happy."

Fear—or was it something else?—zinged through Leigh as Beth opened the door, revealing a foyer with a stone floor and a yawning staircase just beyond.

Adventure. That was what Margot would've said this was, and as Leigh's pulse went wild, she craved it as she'd never craved anything else in her life.

She had a good figure now. She'd been told she was actually pretty after all that weight had come off.

It was time to make the most of what she'd never had.

She stepped across the threshold, breathing in, out, trying to keep her heart in her chest.

As Beth closed the door behind them, Leigh heard a voice just beyond the foyer, to the left.

"Good to see you here, Leigh."

A deep, dark tone.

2

LEIGH HAD EXPECTED to find *him,* Mystery Man, standing there with a saucy grin on his face.

But all she discovered was an antique table holding a small wire stand that propped up a smartphone. Next to it was her auction basket; it was open, exposing blue-and-white-gingham lining, plus the jars of honey she had labeled with each course idea for this date.

Looking at the inside of that basket, she felt as if this man had already undone part of her, like a button on her shirt.

She shivered, especially when he spoke again.

"You took a while to get up here, Leigh."

When she answered him, she tried to control her voice. "Fashionably late, right?"

There had only been a bit of a quaver in her words. Not bad.

"Better you come late than never coming at all," he parried.

Leigh didn't know whether to laugh or melt into a stunned pool of sighs. Had he just tossed a sexual innuendo her way? And did he have any idea how twisted this was? How…

God, how kind of, sort of…okay…*absolutely* intriguing?

She sneaked a glance back at Beth, sending her a nonverbal message. *Seriously? Talking to me through a speaker is part of the date?*

Beth smiled. *This is just the beginning.* Then she walked toward the table and picked up the phone. "How about a quick tour of the place before we head to the kitchen?"

They were trying to get her settled. Not a bad idea, although Leigh wondered if she would ever feel relaxed tonight.

"Sounds good," she said.

She followed Beth back through the foyer and past the grand staircase, all the while keeping her eye on that phone in Beth's hand.

The parlor, or living room, or whatever superrich people called a place like this, was just as expansive as the staircase and foyer. It boasted a wall-wide view of the beach below, the waves rolling toward the shoreline as the sun kept descending. The furnishings reminded Leigh of a leather-, cherrywood- and brass-filled museum.

"How old is this house?" she asked just to make conversation since the phone had been silent.

Mystery Man's voice answered. "It's not as ancient as it seems. It was built to look like old money, but it hasn't been around for more than thirty years."

"I was hoping you'd tell me something like it's been in your family since the Dark Ages. But among other things, I know you don't live here."

As the voice on the phone laughed, even Beth seemed tickled that Leigh was still attempting to unearth information.

Maybe Beth had been right: enjoy the night for what it was, because it sure seemed as if Mr. Millionaire had the means to give her a decadent date. And how many times had she been on one of those?

Sure, she was used to living a better lifestyle now with her show and all. But her date had flown her down here, then offered to put her up in a high-class hotel, which she had refused because it had seemed like *too* much. He seemed to be pretty free with his money.

As Leigh walked around the room, touching the grand piano by the window, then running her hand along the top of the long curved brass-backed sofa, she pictured a man who might go along with the voice. Secretive mogul? Billionaire cowboy?

"Does it bother you," he asked, "that I might know more about you than you know about me?"

"I'd be lying if I said it doesn't." And she'd be lying if she said that it didn't do something to her in a deep, shady place that she'd always repressed. This game he was playing was almost like voyeurism, where he could see her but she couldn't see him.

There was some power in knowing that he was interested in her enough to have singled her out, wasn't there? It was kinky, and made her feel a little audacious. Lord knows, she'd never been audacious with a man before.

She stopped at a vintage brass-trimmed minibar, inspecting it. "What exactly do you know about me?"

"We could start with the superficial," he said. "You've got a cooking show, but before that you were a personal gourmet chef who spent some time in Nashville working for a few country-singing stars. One of them gave you enough clout to get that show of yours going."

"You've done some homework on me."

As they talked, Beth strolled out of the room, leading Leigh to the staircase. It was as if the woman was a butler or maid of sorts in an old black-and-white suspense movie—there but not quite there, silent as a shadow in candlelight.

"Believe it or not, Leigh," he said, "your life is an open book."

Right on Beth's heels, Leigh climbed the stairs slowly, trailing her hand along the polished wood banister. "Why do you say that? What else do you know about me?"

Thud, went her boot on a stair. *Thud,* on another. Just like loud, body-shaking heartbeats.

"At Cal-U," he said, "you were a home-economics major. You were on the board for Rodeo Days each year and on the dean's list, among other honors."

"And?"

His laugh traveled over the air, infiltrating her.

"And I know everything that's on your biography page for the show's website."

Leigh almost missed a step as she came to the top of the stairs to a long hallway lit by iron wall sconces and lined with an Oriental rug.

How *much* did this man know about her? How deep had his research gone?

She tried not to think about painful things, like her struggle to love herself her entire life. Or…

Leigh took a breath. Or like her sister, Hannah, who'd died in a swimming accident before Leigh had even gotten out of high school. Hannah, who always was and would be the perfect child in the eyes of their parents.

Beth was waiting for her at the end of the hallway, which featured a huge circular stained-glass window. She had a concerned look on her face as she watched Leigh, probably wondering if she was so thrown off-balance by this setup that she was about to flee.

But Leigh merely gave her a grin, then kept walking toward the window, which depicted a blue rose surrounded by white panels that resembled shards of ice.

As she surveyed its beauty, she said, "It's too bad you don't actually live here, Mystery Man. The furnishings might've told me something about you."

A drawn-out pause made her chest beat with an anxious rhythm. Was he thinking about telling her his name?

When his voice came back on the line, it was warmer, as if he did know her beyond a superficial biography.

"You can call me Callum," he said. "That should do for now."

Callum. Now it was easier to picture a face—a dark-haired man with wild locks and eyes as blue as the stained-glass rose. A guy who belonged in a Gothic mansion—one who matched this voice.

She went stiff between her legs, her pulse throbbing there. She was truly into this game now, and wondering what the night would bring only pumped her up more.

Beth had been staring at the blue rose, as if she felt uncomfortable being a part of this private discussion between her friend and her fellow sorority sister.

But all Leigh could think was *Callum*. Even if the name he'd given her was fake—which it probably was—she was genuinely hoping the rest of the date could begin now.

She took the phone from Beth, smiling at her with another clear message.

I can take it from here.

Beth didn't show any emotion, just gave a polite smile and left Leigh alone with her Mystery Man.

When Beth had gone down the stairs, the front door shutting behind her, Leigh finally spoke.

"Callum," she said, "can I start cooking now?"

ADAM DIDN'T GO near Leigh until she told him she was ensconced in the kitchen.

He was fairly certain she had no idea that he was nearby, in a darkened alcove that overlooked the cooking area from above. He wondered if she would be freaked out to realize he was within such close proximity of her…or if she would be just as stimulated as he was by this next move in the game that had started with her auction basket.

She had propped the disposable phone on a stand that had been waiting on one of the marble counters along with the high-end cooking accessories he'd had delivered. When Beth had arranged the date, Adam had insisted on stocking up on supplies instead of having Leigh do it, and he hoped he'd gotten everything she needed.

It looked as if he'd done well, though. She was smiling as she inspected the dry ingredients while standing at the kitchen island under the pots and pans hanging above it.

The auction basket stood in the center of the island. Even so, everything seemed to revolve around Leigh, not the basket. She was more beautiful than she was on TV, her blond hair shiny and long as it trailed down her back, pinned away from her face with a simple barrette she'd pulled from her jeans pocket. And dressed in those sexy country clothes, she had his imagination running on all cylinders, pushing steam through him until he felt ready to burst in several key places.

But tonight didn't feel like a tawdry encounter. It felt good just to look at her, be near her. Somehow, looking made the numbness he'd experienced for over two years go away, even just temporarily.

Looking at her brought back a time before his life had crashed down all around him, not just once with his dad's death but twice with his wife's.

Leigh seemed content to play along with his setup as she washed her hands, then dried them.

He spoke into his own disposable cell phone and leaned back against a wall, not moving, never giving himself away.

"How about you open up that honey wine that's still in the fridge?"

She glanced at the phone, and for a moment he felt a little envious that *it* was getting all the attention, not "Callum," the name he'd given her. It'd been his paternal grandfather's name and safe enough that it wouldn't provide a strong connection if she should pop it into a computer to do some research on him.

"That wine's for after dinner," she said, moving over to the fridge and taking out a bottle of Chardonnay. "But I like a nip or two of the drier stuff while I'm cooking, so don't mind if I do."

"You don't drink on your show."

"Producer's choice. They don't want to encourage reckless cooking."

She smiled as she poured herself a glass, then lifted it in a toast.

"To you, wherever you are."

She tipped her glass to all four corners of the room, and when she got to where he was hidden, he went even stiller than before, as if she had somehow discovered him.

But that was ridiculous. And it was heart-poundingly exciting to feel as if he'd almost gotten caught.

She took a sip, then set down the glass, reaching for one of her honey jars and unscrewing the lid. He knew that she was going to give him his money's worth with some corn bread, a salad, balsamic honey–glazed lamb chops, spicy honey-roasted cauliflower and, ultimately, a honeycomb cake.

An impetuous thought kicked him: What would she do if he appeared down there by her side to eat dinner with her?

The notion made his chest feel as if it had closed right up. He wouldn't be showing himself. He liked this so-called date as it was—flirting, seduction by shadow, no responsibilities in the end, just as if he were on the computer having yet another virtual encounter.

Maybe, as Beth said, he *was* warped.

Leigh had turned on the oven and was now greasing a pan for the bread.

"So what's with you and Beth?" she said, a lilt in her voice.

She was flirting with him. He couldn't be wrong about that, because little by little, as she had taken a tour of this house, he'd sensed her warming up to his voice.

"Beth is a friend—" he started to say.

"I know, I know." She put the bread pan aside and

cleaned her hands. "Friends and professional associates. But she's a beautiful woman, too. Don't you ever…?"

His shields went up at the mere suggestion of a romantic relationship with anyone. "No. Never."

Leigh's posture stiffened.

Recovering, he said, "First, Beth is like a big sister to me. Second, she's not into my type."

Leigh seized on that. "What type is that?"

He smiled at her perseverance. "Men."

Leigh's mouth formed an O. But then she went right back to cooking, measuring flour in a cup and dumping it into the bowl. "That's funny, because when Beth showed up at the auction and bid on my basket, everyone thought…you know…that *she* was bidding on me."

"Under any other circumstances, that could've been the case. But she considers herself unlucky in love and hasn't been serious about anyone for a while. There's just too much work to do for me, she says. Supposedly, the hours she puts in make it hard to find a meaningful relationship."

"You sound like quite a taskmaster."

"I'm not the one who keeps her at her desk overtime. She's a workaholic."

By now Leigh had poured the cornmeal into the bowl. "You met her back in college? When you were a Phi Rho Mu brother and she was a Tau Epsilon Gamma sister?"

Leigh sure wasn't shy about digging for information, no matter how many brick walls she ran into.

"We crossed paths briefly at Cal-U." He wasn't going to tell Leigh that Beth had been born and raised in a town near his and that he'd met her only once at a party during pledging but had found her résumé online later.

That had been five years ago, just after he'd gotten married.

After adding sugar and baking powder to the bowl, Leigh asked, "What were you like in school?"

"You really think I'm going to answer that?"

"I had to give it a shot." She laughed and made a well in the center of the dry ingredients. Every move captured his attention, enchanting him, especially with that country-girl blouse she was wearing—the one that gave him a tempting peek of cleavage and tanned stomach.

"Do you have black hair?" she asked. "Because that's how I'm picturing you. A very Callum-like dark Irish guy, like Riley Donahue but a bit more roguish. Remember Riley? Nice guy, ag-business major?"

"I heard through the grapevine that he's engaged to Danielle Hughes."

"See, you were around the university when I was."

He didn't confirm or deny. "You've got the color of my hair right, at least. I'll give you that much."

"Good. Sounds like I'm finally getting somewhere."

Her happiness made him want to give her more, but he would no doubt regret giving her too much.

She was on a roll, though. "What do you do for a living?"

"I invite women over to rental houses and watch them cook. It's a fetish."

She really laughed at that, and he realized that she was sincerely enjoying herself.

And him. And this date. She wasn't afraid of either one. In fact, he was bringing joy to a woman when he hadn't done so for a long, long time, and he was doing it with only his voice.

But, again, this whole thing was temporary, and he had to keep that in mind.

After her laugh trailed off, a seemingly endless pause reigned. Was it because she realized that he'd used the word *fetish?* She'd given him a similar hesitation earlier when he'd laid that opening line on her—a thinly veiled allusion to coming.

But he'd only been testing her when she'd entered the house, seeing how much she was going to take from him. He'd probably been doing the same thing just now, too. Hell, he'd even been doing it during the house tour when he had told her what he knew about her. He could've pushed her further by mentioning her deceased sister, but he hadn't wanted to bring up any ghosts like Hannah. And certainly not his wife, Carla.

Was he trying to unnerve Leigh, getting her to leave before she could decide to do so on her own?

But she was still here, stirring heavy cream, vegetable oil, honey and eggs into that bowl.

She said, "You know what's funny about this date?"

Besides everything? "What?"

"It's not that you're talking to me on a phone or that you're playing around with me by not showing yourself. It's a cat-and-mouse game, and believe it or not, I get that."

"So what's so funny?"

She poured the batter into the pan. "Do you ever think that it's easier to talk to someone you can't see?"

He narrowed his gaze, hoping she'd go on.

She didn't disappoint. "A few years ago there was a vendor I used for my produce. We used to talk on the phone all the time for business. But then our talks started to get…"

"Suggestive?" It was almost a whisper.

"Yeah. But only mildly." She stopped pouring and looked at the phone, as if it truly were him. "Our talking never went anywhere, and all I knew of him was his voice. But somehow I felt like *he* knew a part of me that no one else did, just because nobody else had ever made me feel like he did before, merely by chatting with me."

"How did he make you feel?"

She thought about it for a moment, then said, "As if I might be able to suggest something to him that I would never say in person, if that makes any sense. I never did that, though. After he shut down his business, I never talked to him again."

As she put the pan in the oven, he thought he saw a yearning on her face that was so acute he wanted to make it go away.

It was at that moment he knew there were a lot of stories Leigh could tell him, a lot of mysteries about her that he'd like to solve.

Had he fallen in love—or lust—at first sight with her back in college at that party? Or maybe he was a fool who could indulge that lost sentimental part of him only here, in the near darkness.

Either way, he wanted more.

"When do you need to leave town?" he asked without thinking.

She'd been wiping off the counter, and she stopped. "I'm on hiatus from my show...."

As she let the words hang, he got the feeling that she just might be open to coming back for a second date if the rest of the night went well...if he didn't put any pressure on her and they merely had dinner, with him still at a distance, still playing the game.

And if he gave her something to come back for.

THIS WAS DEFINITELY a date that would go down in the Singlehood Hall of Fame.

After Leigh had finished preparing the rest of the dinner, she had expected Callum to come-out-come-out-wherever-he-was.

But…no.

He had asked her to set aside his meal in the oven for later and to fix a plate for herself so she could take it to the dining room, where a long mahogany table was already set.

Low light from a chandelier toasted the room as she sat down with her plate and her glass of wine. She placed the phone on another stand that was waiting at a setting next to hers.

What was Callum's agenda? Yeah, she knew he must have planned some sort of scenario, but surely it couldn't last all night. Or maybe he was gauging how far he could take this. She'd seen that movie *9½ Weeks,* and she knew that there were men out there who didn't do paint-by-number relationships or dates.

Was he one of them?

Another delicious shiver danced over her skin. What did it say about *her* that she wanted to see how far he would push this thing? And why did she want to start pushing it herself?

She leaned back in her chair, holding the wine in front of her as the aroma of all her honeyed dishes tickled her senses. She glanced around the room, wondering where he was, feeling the voyeuristic thrill of this game once again. It wasn't all that different from being on TV, knowing people would be watching you, never being able to see their expressions.

Let's see…. There was a darkened second story mezzanine rimming the room. Was he up there? Somewhere?

"Is there a peephole or something that you're using?" she asked.

"No." His laugh filled the phone speaker. "You make me sound like a bad man in a horror movie, Leigh."

"Bad in what way?"

Their conversations so far hadn't crossed any boundaries, but she knew that she'd just put out an invitation to do some testing.

"I'm not sure I should answer that."

"Why?"

"Because I'm not sure how much bad you can take. You were always a nice girl, weren't you?"

"Isn't that why you bid on my basket?"

He chuckled again, and she decided that it was really time to push back.

Putting down her wine, she leaned forward, resting her elbows on the table as she idly picked up a piece of bread. She'd set a bowl of honey nearby, and she dipped into it, letting the thick liquid drip.

"What kind of girl," she said, her pulse tripping, "offers up the kind of basket I did to a total stranger?"

"Ah, but that was the genius of your basket. It was innocent, but…"

He trailed off when she took the bread and held it a few inches above her mouth, drizzling honey into it. Some of the liquid meandered over her lips, and she licked at it, then took a tiny nibble of bread.

Her chin was sticky with the stuff, too, but she let it stay there for now.

"You were saying?" she asked, barely recognizing her husky tone.

But she was delighting in the freedom of this night, being the only person in this room, with him far enough away that she wouldn't have to see his face and know whether or not she was acting like a complete and utter fool.

Somehow she got the feeling that she didn't look like an idiot at all—that he *was* enjoying the show.

She put down her bread, casually wiping off the stray honey from her chin, then sucking it from her finger. He'd stayed silent this entire time.

"You were talking about how innocent my basket was?" she asked.

His voice sounded gritty now. "It appeared that way at first."

"And now?"

"Now," he said, "I'm not sure what you're about."

She was actually good at seduction. Who knew?

She took it up another notch. "Turnabout is fair play, because I have no idea what you're about, either."

After rubbing her finger over her bottom lip, she used her tongue to coyly lick off more honey from that finger. He muttered something on the other end of the phone, and it sounded like an amused curse.

Good. Let him be just as thwarted as she'd been this whole time.

"You know," she said, forgoing the rest of her meal and dipping her finger into the honey bowl this time, swirling the thick mass around, "I have to wonder why you won't just come out here and sit with me. Is it because I do know who you are and you're afraid I'm going to get turned off?"

"Why would you say that?"

"If you were someone I didn't like in the fraternity, then it would make sense that you'd rather keep your distance and just play around with me from afar. It would be a sort of revenge for you."

A pause, then, "You didn't know me. No one really did." His words sounded ominous until he followed them up with, "Besides, I don't think you disliked anyone."

She scooped out more honey, bringing it over to her plate, where she laved the bread with it just as if it were…well, not bread at all but a part of him.

As she smoothed the honey back and forth with sensual strokes, she smiled. "Is there something about you that's unlikable?"

"I'm only a man who's very happy with the way this date is going so far. That's all."

"And how is this date going?"

He didn't say anything for a moment, as if he was content with merely watching her play with the honey. As if he was imagining her finger on him, sliding back and forth, making him heat up.

Just the thought of getting a rise out of Callum sent prickles of desire through her, a wash of passion, coating her with thick dampness.

"This date is going perfectly," he finally said.

"You like that I'm up for entertaining you?" *Bold,* she thought. *And it feels awesome.*

"I wouldn't exactly reduce you to just being the entertainment."

She took a different tack. "Why did you wonder when I'm going to be heading home, Callum?"

As she waited for a response, she pictured him as a lonely man. Or was he the opposite—someone who merely had a rich fantasy life that he didn't want anyone to know about?

He spoke. "Beth might have mentioned to you that I'm vacationing here for the time being."

"She did." A tingle got her right in the belly. Did he have more plans for her? She laughed softly, helping him along. "Do you need a cook or something?"

"Not exactly, although you're killing me with the smell of this meal."

Good God—he *was* somewhere close. "Then come down here and eat it."

"Later."

Was he stringing her along, promising he was going to reveal himself if she came back another night? Lord help her, but she was so damned curious about him that she would return here again and again until she saw his face.

His voice was as smooth as the honey she'd been playing with when he came back on the phone. "What are you doing tomorrow night?"

Nothing. But she wasn't about to let him know that so easily. "I'll have to look at my social calendar."

"Then we'll see if you're free, and I'll be in touch."

And with that, he was gone, leaving her with a meal that she was too excited—and too calorie conscious—to eat.

Leaving her with the sense that, finally, after all these years, she could be as free as she wanted to be if she returned for some more playtime with her Mystery Man.

3

DANI COULDN'T WAIT a minute more to find out what was happening with Leigh, even if her friend might still be in the middle of her date.

Fifteen minutes ago she'd gotten off a catering job in Tulare, where she and Riley rented a house. The gig was for the same outfit she'd been with for years now—although she longed for the day when she could open her own small company. She'd headed directly for the lingerie shop nearby, browsing the massage oil and accessory section, but the whole time, she'd been obsessing about checking on Leigh. After all, what if the date was going badly? What if her friend needed an emergency call to end the night?

She decided to compromise with a text.
You good?

Dani didn't get an answer right away, so she drove the short distance from the boutique to her little stucco home with its trimmed lawn, perennial flowers and bird fountain. Riley's truck was in the drive, and she grasped her pink shopping bag and rushed into the house to see him.

Since he'd had the day off from his small-estate management job, he had prepped steaks for dinner, plus a salad, sautéed mushrooms and French bread. It all waited on the kitchen table for her. But when she saw her fiancé, his dark hair tousled, his blue eyes bright as he smiled at her, she dropped her bag and ran into his arms.

"Dinner smells great," she said, nestling her face in his neck as she stood on her tiptoes. He always smelled so good, too, like laundry detergent. Clean and fresh.

He kissed the top of her head and murmured, "I was just about to put the steaks on."

"You sure they can't wait?" She drew back from him and dangled the pink shopping bag.

At first Riley got a look on his face that she'd grown all too used to since she'd been doing a lot of lingerie shopping after their fraternity/sorority reunion. She wouldn't say it was sadness, exactly. Maybe just a second of resignation, of thinking that he missed the sweet, docile girl she used to be before she'd had her epiphany about being stronger and more adventurous.

Just as Margot had been with her basket, and now Leigh.

And maybe Dani *had* gone a bit off the deep end. She had taken a good look at herself after her friends had arranged that basket auction to raise money for the big wedding she'd wanted ever since she was a child. The one she and Riley couldn't afford these days.

It was just that her friends' gesture had rubbed her the wrong way. Had everyone always looked at Dani as if she was helpless? And how much longer was she going to be able to live with that?

So she'd decided that it was high time to grow up—to become a success like Margot and Leigh, not the contented former home-ec major who worked for a catering company she didn't even own. Although she still had to work for someone else for a while, she planned to open her own catering outfit soon.

Best of all, she had started jazzing up her sex life with Riley, inspired by Margot's steamy basket and how much it had turned on Clint Barrows, who was now the love of her life.

Dani and Riley never looked at each other the way Margot and Clint did. Why not? Dani had wondered. Why couldn't *they* have combustible chemistry like that?

When she had started nudging Riley into more exotic intimate situations, he'd been surprised at first, wondering if she was just suffering from cold feet before their upcoming wedding. Wondering if she was freaking out because her parents had gotten a terrible divorce several years ago and she feared turning out exactly like them.

But he had decided that they should get to know each other all over again. He wanted to "court" her. It was a fairly sweet word for what they'd been doing.

Just as Riley was about to say something in response to her pink shopping bag, her phone rang.

"It's got to be Leigh," she said, dropping her purchases.

Riley merely smiled at her, then went to the patio door, no doubt to get their steaks going.

Dani watched him leave, her heart fisting in her chest as the phone rang again. She was going to make him happy tonight—and for the rest of their lives. She just had to figure out how to feel happy herself.

When he was gone, she grabbed her phone, looked at the ID screen, then put the call on speakerphone. "Are you alive?" she asked.

Leigh laughed. "No, I'm coming at you from the Other Side. Boo!"

"Stop it. I was just worried about you."

"You shouldn't have been. I'm outside Mystery Man's house by the gate, waiting for Margot to pick me up."

"And...?"

Leigh's voice lowered. "It was...different."

"How?"

"First off, he never showed himself to me."

Why did Dani's thoughts immediately go to somewhere horny? Probably because of what was in her pink bag.

"Do you mean that he kept being Mystery Man?" she asked. "The whole night?"

"That's exactly what I mean."

Dani started to hum the *Twilight Zone* theme until Leigh shushed her.

"The situation really wasn't as oddball as it sounds." Leigh skipped a beat. "I think."

"You sound as confused as I am."

"It's just that I got used to the way he was running things. After Beth brought me up to the house, I did meet him. Sort of. He was on a phone."

Dani frowned. "That's how it stayed the entire time? With him talking to you on an electronic device?"

"It was fun. Like...phone sex. I don't know how to explain it."

"You guys had phone sex?"

"No." Leigh laughed again. "He watched me cook dinner as we chatted—"

"Did he have a TV to watch you on? Is that how he was keeping an eye on you?" This was getting kookier by the second.

"I'm not sure how he was watching me. Anyway, after I cooked, I ate the dinner."

"By yourself."

"Right. Actually, I didn't eat. I wasn't very hungry."

It was probably a rich meal anyway, and Dani knew that Leigh was always watching her intake. "Did he eat?"

"Not with me. A good way to put it is that while I was at the table, I ate the most of the honey and some bread while he watched me from wherever he was."

Dani sucked in a breath, then whispered, "You did food sex?"

"I won't get into details, but it actually was fun. And I think it was the first time I ever had any real fun on a date. Usually, you just go through the motions with a guy, trying to impress him, trying to be polite and not get food between your teeth or look like a pig at dinner. Boring as hell, right? Until now."

Dani sat in a nearby chair. "You liked it. You're into some kink and you never even knew it."

Leigh got a teasing tone to her voice. "Maybe you're right. Because I'm going back there."

"You're *what?*"

"I said I'm going back. I think. He pretty much invited me to the house again at the end of dinner."

Riley ambled into the room with a plate of steaks in hand. Dani took in the aroma, along with the smell of mushrooms that already permeated the kitchen.

He nodded toward the phone. "Hey, Leigh, are you still alive or did the boogeyman get you?"

"Hah-hah," Leigh said. "You two must share thoughts as well as everything else."

He set the steaks down and began to put them on two

plates. "I'm just checking up on you. We'd kind of like to have you around, in one piece."

"That's sweet, Riley." Leigh changed topic. "Oh— here's Margot. Talk to you all soon, okay?"

Dani shook a finger at the phone. "You be careful when you go back there."

"Yeah, yeah."

They signed off, leaving Dani and Riley at the table, alone at last.

He glanced at the pink bag on the floor but didn't say anything about it as he sat, opening a bottle of beer for her, then one for him.

"I'm not even going to ask what happened on that date," he said.

Even though she and Riley shared everything—as Leigh had pointed out—Dani hesitated to tell him the details of the night. They were just too...

She was about to say "insane," but then she got that flippy-floppy turn of the stomach, telling her that Leigh's date had actually captured her imagination.

Phone sex. A dark stranger.

Dani bypassed her steak and beer, pulling her chair closer to Riley's and grabbing her pink bag on the way.

"Do you think we could hold off on the steak and take a little break before dinner?" she asked.

This time, instead of that sadness in his gaze, she detected a spark. And when she brought out the pair of blue fuzzy handcuffs she'd purchased, he put down his beer.

She got out of her chair and went to an odds-and-ends drawer near the oven, taking out a length of blue fabric she occasionally used to decorate the center of the table. She showed it to him.

"I wonder," she said, "how it felt when Leigh realized that her date wasn't going to show her who he was tonight."

Riley cocked a brow. "He did what?"

"Long story." She went over to him, then trailed the material over his shoulder. "I want to know what it feels like to have some mystery going on with us, Riley."

He grabbed the material, wrapping it around his hand, and she knew that they'd started some courting.

Not long ago, when she had told Riley that she wanted to push their boundaries in the bedroom, he had asked her if she was unhappy in their relationship. She wasn't. Hadn't ever been.

But there were so many things she hadn't enjoyed in life yet. Would she regret never exploring those things before they got married and then realize years down the road that it was too late?

She sat on his lap, snuggling her butt toward his groin, which was already straining against his button fly.

"Blindfold me," she said.

He looked at the steaks, as practical a man as ever, until she cupped his chin with a hand and made him focus on her.

"Those can wait," she said, already sounding like the type of woman who would go into a dark house to meet a dark man.

He grinned, and it wasn't a carefree Riley grin, either. It was a hungry one, and it shocked her deep in her groin.

As he slid a hand up her ribs, over her breast, on his way to grab the material, she gasped. Then, almost roughly, he turned her around on his lap.

He wrapped the material to cover her eyes, tying it

securely. "This is what you want?" he asked in a gruff voice.

He didn't sound like himself, either, and her blood pushed through her veins as she tried to match the voice with her image of him. But even blindfolded, she still saw Riley.

She pointed toward the cuffs on the table. "You'll want to make sure I can't take off this blindfold."

"Why?"

"Because even though you don't want me to know your identity, I'm dying to see who you are." Or who he was going to play at being.

She'd meant it teasingly, but was he thinking that she should know who he was by now? It felt as if a piece of her heart had crumbled because she wasn't sure just how invested he was in all these games she was introducing.

Was she seeing how far he would go before he left her? Would she be getting a divorce from him before they were married thirty-seven years just like her parents had been, saving them the time and heartache?

As she felt Riley reach for the handcuffs, she remembered the first time she had seen him, during a party. He'd been leaning against the outside wall of the fraternity house by the pool with some friends, smiling and drinking a soda, and she had thought what a nice guy he probably was. She'd been a freshman who didn't know much about boys, and she and Riley had ended up friends. It'd only been after college that she had met up with him again and the fireworks had started.

It had been smooth sailing ever since…until now, when she felt the handcuffs close around her wrists.

She turned her face to him, forgetting for a moment that she couldn't see him from under the blindfold.

"This is how you want it?" he asked again.

She nodded, and he stood, taking her by the waist at the same time, then putting her on the chair and raising her hands above her head. She rested her palms on her head, feeling vulnerable, her breasts pushing against her sweater.

As her pulse flailed, he pulled up her skirt, and her first instinct was to close her legs. But he guided them back open.

Heat sang through her, but so did a little bit of fear, as her clit throbbed in anticipation.

"Do you like not being able to see me, Dani?" he asked. "Is this dangerous for you?"

"It's safe enough." Always safe with Riley.

At least, that was what she thought until he slipped his hand between her legs, touching her at her most sensitive point.

She made a desperate sound, and he tugged her panties away from her body. Air tickled her.

"Who am I tonight?" he asked, and she detected a trace of that sadness in him again. "Who do you want me to be?"

"I…"

She wanted to say "Riley," but that didn't go along with the dark-man fantasy.

When he eased his fingers between her legs and strummed her, she breathed in and clamped her arms around her head. He put his mouth close to her ear, and when he spoke, she startled.

"You need to think about who you really want, Dani," he said softly.

Was he saying that she needed to name an identity

for him so that the fantasy would work? Or was there something more important he wanted her to think about?

She bit her lip as he worked her with his fingers, pushing her toward a place where, hopefully, she was going to see the light.

DURING THE CAR ride to the Sea Breeze Suites where Margot and Leigh were staying for a couple of nights, Leigh answered every question Margot had about the date. Even when they'd gotten back to their room, camped out on their beds while hardly able to even think about getting to sleep yet, Margot didn't stop her inquisition.

"Really?" she asked for about the twentieth time. "You're going on another date with him?"

The more Margot disbelieved her, the more determined Leigh was to have her next encounter with Callum.

Leigh Vaughn, with her skinny jeans and a whole new attitude. She hadn't realized how boring her life was until tonight, when she'd experienced a little bit of adventure.

And craved more.

"You bet I'm going back," she said. "And you know what? If he can play a game with me, I can play just as well. You should've seen me at dinner with the honey. You would've been proud."

Seemingly persuaded, Margot leaned back against the pillows she'd propped against the headboard. Then she smiled like a well-fed cat. "Leigh has arrived."

Was that a blush she felt creeping up her face?

Nah. Women who flirted with unknown men didn't blush.

After kicking off her hand-tooled red boots and putting her feet on the mattress, she leaned back against the headboard, too.

"I've been asking myself one question since I left," she said. "What kind of man invites over a well-known cook he somehow knew from college and cuts out of the date as if his house is on fire?"

"You really want me to answer that?" In the car, Margot had compared Callum to everyone from Count Dracula to the Marquis de Sade. You just never knew, she said. But now she sighed. "I was on the computer while you were gone, conducting another search of Phi Rho Mu. But there're no millionaires who matched the name Callum."

"Whoever he is, I think he's kind of shy."

"Shy? Some of the things he said to you—especially that opening line about coming—aren't the stuff shy men say."

"Playing a game can make a person brassier than they usually are." Leigh thought about the moment she'd licked the honey off her fingers and when she'd spread it over the bread with suggestive slowness. "I know that having him in the shadows did something to *me*. It gave me some…"

"Power?"

"Yeah." Leigh turned her head so she could look at Margot. "I've never had power before."

"Yes, you have. You've got a TV show. You're a rising star, Leigh. That's some power."

"Business is different."

They were both quiet for a moment. In fact, Margot seemed too quiet. And she had that expression on her face that she got whenever she and Leigh talked about their jobs.

Enough was enough. "What's going on with you, Marg?"

It must've been the compassionate tone of her voice, because Margot closed her eyes, then put on an embarrassed smile.

"I was going to tell you sometime or another. Might as well be now."

"Is everything okay?"

"More than okay. In most ways." She tucked a dark strand of hair behind her ear. "Do you know why I'm not writing the 'single woman on the go' books anymore?"

Something was already sinking inside Leigh's chest. "No."

Margot shrugged. "My publisher canceled my last contract. Sales were declining, they said."

"Oh, Margot." Leigh sat away from the headboard.

She held up a hand. "No pity, please. Don't they say that when a door closes on you, a window opens? Well, that's what happened with this new blog and the 'city girl goes country' book I'm working on. You know the blog's getting a lot of hits, and maybe that could lead to another publisher buying a book or two. And then there's Clint." Margot got a dreamy look in her eyes. "He's the best opened window of all."

"So life is good?"

"How can it not be with him around? Everything's great, including the fact that his brothers, who were about to sue the pants off of him because he didn't want to sell the cutting-horse ranch, have backed down now that we've got a bulldog lawyer on our side."

Leigh leaned against the headboard again, smiling at her friend.

Margot returned the gesture. "Know what the worst part of all this was, though?"

"What?"

"Telling you that I'd failed."

Leigh knit her brows, about to argue, but Margot went on.

"We've had this competitive thing going on since college. Last month you even told me that you've always wanted to be just like me, and that everything came so easily to me."

Leigh remembered. They'd been in a bridal shop, perusing gowns for Dani. She had gotten a pang that day—the sense that she would probably never get married because her inner chubby girl kept telling her no man would want her in the long run, after she inevitably gained all her weight back. She'd told Margot that she more or less envied her because Margot had always been the perfect one, but then her friend had gotten that expression on her face....

Now Leigh understood the reason.

"In my eyes," she said to Margot, "you're always going to be a winner. Look at how you've bounced back already."

Margot smiled, and she was just about to say something when Leigh's cell phone rang.

They looked at each other, gazes wide.

"Well?" Margot said, nearly bursting. "Are you going to get that or what?"

Leigh promised to talk to Margot later as she grabbed the phone and peered at the ID screen.

"It's Beth Dahrling," she said, her pulse whipping into a frenzy again, just before she pushed the answer button.

WHEN ADAM RECEIVED Beth's Skype call on his computer that night, he was in his bedroom near the attic of the mansion, a room that hadn't been included in Leigh's tour.

He pushed aside the quarterly projections for one of the biofuel companies he'd invested in and focused on Beth instead.

She was wearing a silk dressing gown, her hair in a bun at her nape, as she sat at a desk in the guest cottage on the mansion's property. "I just thought you might want to know that Leigh officially said yes to tomorrow."

Adam sat back in his chair, smiling. He'd been trying to steady his heartbeat for the past couple of hours while wondering if Leigh would sincerely want to have a second encounter with "Callum." He'd ended the date so abruptly that he thought he might've made a mistake in trying to leave her with her curiosity about him intact.

"You'll make arrangements for a limousine to pick her up at her hotel tomorrow?" he asked.

"Yes, and I told her where to wait on the beach below the mansion after she's dropped off. After your date, it'll be taking her back to her hotel, too."

"She'll be here just in time to enjoy the sunset."

He had a little something planned—slow seduction, heated suggestion, sweet words on a phone as she strolled down the shoreline much as she'd strolled through his rented mansion tonight, flirting with him.... He wasn't sure what would come after that, though.

All he knew was that he had to see her again. Hear her voice, her laugh.

Beth reached for the keyboard as if to terminate the connection.

"Wait," he said. "You're not still angry with me."

"*Angry* isn't the word." She looked away from the computer, offscreen.

"Then what's going on with you?"

Her jaw tightened, and he could tell he was in for it.

"We've known each other a fairly long time, Adam," she said, still unwilling to meet his computer gaze. "I didn't know you in college—you weren't there long enough for that—but you were still young when you and Carla hired me to manage your business affairs."

"My late twenties wasn't that young. Especially after what I'd gone through when Dad died." And a few years later, he'd felt even older after watching how much Carla had suffered with the damned cancer.

"Believe it or not," Beth said, finally looking into the computer's eye, "you were different back then. You were...normal."

The word struck him. "Normal?"

"You actually had the capacity to feel. You wouldn't have shut yourself away and screwed with a woman's head like you did tonight...and like you're probably going to do tomorrow. Unless I'm wrong and you're going to be Adam Morgan with her."

A short laugh escaped him. "What's normal anyway?"

Was it setting yourself up like a target and waiting for life to shoot bullets at you? Was it taking those bullets and pretending that they hadn't ripped you apart? Or was "normal" the opposite—putting on layers and layers of protection just so you could make sure you never got hit again?

Beth was shaking her head. "Don't ever ask me what normal is, Adam. I might not have the definition, but I know it's not this. And I don't think for a minute that this Callum act is going to make you happy in the end. As I told you earlier, someone's going to get burned in your little game, and I'm pretty sure it's not going to be you."

He bristled. "Overly concerned for Leigh, are we?"

"She was one of my sorority sisters and in general she's a nice person. I don't like to see people hurt." She tilted her head. "I don't like to see you hurting, either."

At that moment, he wished he could be different, if only for Beth's sake. But he liked being this way, didn't he? Or maybe he just had to be this way to tolerate what life dealt out.

"Truthfully," Beth said, drawing her robe around her tighter, "I'm surprised Leigh is going for this."

He was, too, but he didn't say so.

Beth lifted up her hands in a "who can figure it out?" gesture. "I guess you must have caught her at the right time. She lost all that weight, and I can tell you that as a woman, even taking off five pounds makes you feel like a goddess. She's feeling that with Callum, I suppose."

"Leigh's a big girl, and she knows what she wants," he said. "Tonight she flirted with Callum. It was good for both of us. Why ruin it when there's only going to be one more date?"

Beth merely nodded, looking so tired. He sensed a surrender, as if she had no idea what to say to him anymore.

But she might as well have been telling him that Carla wouldn't have known who he was. His wife wouldn't have recognized Adam in the guise of Callum at all.

As he and Beth said good-night and ended their connection, Adam tried to get his mind back on work, but

4

THE LIMOUSINE DROPPED Leigh off near a gate at the foot of the driveway that led to Callum's rented seaside mansion, and she donned her white sweater just before she got out of the backseat.

The uniformed driver beat her to the door. She was an older woman in a suit, her hair pulled back in a gray bun and light pink lipstick her only note of color. As Leigh got out, the driver handed her a phone.

Probably a disposable one, knowing the lengths Callum went to in order to maintain his privacy.

"From your host," the woman said, nodding in farewell. "You have a good night, miss."

Leigh squashed the urge to ask if the driver knew who'd hired her, but she was sure Beth Dahrling would've kept her boss's identity private just like everything else.

"Thank you," she said, accepting the phone. No doubt Callum was going to call her to tell her what would come next. All she'd been told by Beth last night was that she'd be picked up in a limo at the hotel and then she needed to wait on the beach.

But Leigh didn't mind the lack of information. It

made this brief game she and Callum were playing that much more interesting. And, hell, when she went back to her ho-hum real life, she'd be grateful for "interesting."

Going to work, coming home or to whatever hotel she was staying at for the show, going over scripts, going back to work… She hadn't known how much she'd been missing out on until she'd had a glimpse of something much different last night.

The driver gestured toward the bougainvillea-lined beach gate, and Leigh went through it, walking on a path that brought her to a quiet stretch of sand and the murmuring of waves.

As she headed toward the water, she pulled her sweater tighter. The mild November evening wasn't that cold, though. So why was she shivering deep in her belly?

Because she was excited. Nervous. Just as worked up as a girl on her first date—one who had no idea what to expect from a guy. She hadn't slept last night because she'd kept reliving their date over and over, smiling as she lay in bed, hearing Callum's sexy voice echo through the mansion and through her, too. Even now her arms got goose bumps as she remembered his low, mysterious tone, just as thick and sinful as the honey she'd used to make dinner for him.

But everything about him was darker than honey. So much darker. And it was almost as if last night's date had never ended, wrapping itself into this one.

They'd had their foreplay. Bring on whatever came next.

The sun almost looked like honey as it set over the rolling ocean, drizzling down the sky in shades of gold, blue and orange. A few seagulls winged overhead toward the craggy cliff. Up above, she recognized the graceful stone exterior of Callum's rental mansion, and she wondered if he was at a window watching for her. Wondered if his hair really would be black, as she'd imagined. Or if his eyes were that Irish-blue she'd pictured. If he was tall and muscled, or maybe—

The phone rang, and she stopped in her tracks, staring at the cell as the vibrations of sound danced up her arm. It was him.

Whoever "him" really was.

Looking up at his mansion, she took a deep breath, making sure he didn't see how anxious she was, then answered the call. "Enjoying the view?"

He greeted her with a soft laugh that sent ripples of pleasure all through her, settling between her legs. How could he do that to her with just a laugh?

"I'm very much enjoying it," he said.

"You've got a perfect view of the sunset."

"I wasn't talking about that."

She absently tugged at the bottom of her big sweater, which covered most of the country cotton dress she'd chosen for tonight. It was light blue, breezy, almost innocent except for the way the hem fluttered to the middle of her thighs, hinting at sauciness. She was wearing a pair of below-the-knee leather cowgirl boots to go with it.

He spoke again. "You look beautiful, Leigh."

Right. She still looked like a country girl, except with a bit of shine on her. "That's nice of you to say."

A pause stretched over the line. Then, "If I didn't know better, I would say you're not used to compliments."

She shrugged. The people who worked on her cooking show complimented her enough: the makeup artist, the stylist, the director. But she'd always figured it was their job to make her look good.

It could be that Callum was right about how she took compliments, though. It was just that, she'd never been the gorgeous one. She'd never been in first place for anything. That distinction had always belonged to someone else, like her older sister, Hannah, before that fateful day she'd gone for her last swim at a summer party. And then there'd been Margot in college, leaving Leigh in the dust again when it came to looks as well as accomplishments—at least until last night, when Margot had confessed that she wasn't Miss Perfect anymore, what with losing her latest book contract.

But Margot was never a loser, and she would end up even more perfect in the end. Just wait and see. Hannah had been like that, too, and Leigh had done nothing but admire them both, wanting to emulate them, always trying her best to keep up.

Then, by some hormonal miracle, she'd lost her baby fat recently, and that was when she'd realized that maybe she could be in first place, too.

That didn't mean she wanted to ruin this date and talk about life epiphanies with Callum, though.

She made a show of glancing around the abandoned beach. "Not much of a crowd here."

"This is a secluded stretch, and it's not tourist season right now. That's why it's so peaceful."

"Are you coming down to join me?"

"Once again," he said with a chuckle, "good try."

She looked back up at the mansion—its blank windows, its imposing facade, its secrets. "I half expected to see a makeshift kitchen set up down here so I could cook you some beach food this time around."

"We'll get to the food, and the good news is that you'll have the night off."

"I liked cooking for you."

"And I liked eating your meal after you left."

If there was one thing she'd always done well, it was cook. The scales had always testified to that.

She brushed off the thought, knowing that Callum was watching her as she was right now—pounds lighter, with the breeze blowing her skirt around her much slimmer thighs. She felt impulsive. Totally revved up and ready for more adventure right *now*.

"So," she said. "Are you telling me that you'll be cooking for me this time?"

"I've prepared something."

"Nothing too decadent I hope. I splurged enough last night."

"You hardly ate anything."

"Calories add up, you know."

He got quiet again, then said, "The last thing I want you to do is think about what you can and can't have. Promise me that."

Raising her eyebrows, she decided not to comment. Most guys didn't understand what it was like to constantly watch their weight. Damned if she would ever put all those pounds back on.

His next words rocked her. "You've always been the prettiest woman in the room, Leigh. Don't you know that?"

Her skin burned with the compliment, but she still wasn't used to it. He was only buttering her up, right?

"Thanks," she said, grinning, starting to walk along

the shore while the waves reached toward her, then pulled back with a hiss of foam on sand.

"You don't believe me," he said.

It was time for levity again. "Maybe I would if you'd tell me the exact circumstances under which you've seen me before, Callum...."

"Your persistence is entertaining."

"Hey, that's what I do for a living. Entertain people. Have them watch my every televised move."

The air seemed to grow sultrier at her comment. Was it because he didn't respond right away? Or was it because she liked the thought of being watched by *him,* entertaining him even now as delicious tingles gnawed at her?

It was as if he could read her mind. "What does it feel like?" he asked. "Being in front of the camera, never knowing who's watching?"

"Good question." She came to a stop, allowing the breeze to keep playing with her short hem, hoping he was getting a rise out of the subtle, flirty motion. The extended verbal foreplay was getting to her, and she wondered if there'd ever be more than just this.

But she was also mulling over his question. What *was* it like to be in front of the camera? She'd never really thought about it that much, but in this moment, she realized that she'd always wanted to be looked at. And now that she had a new body, new confidence, it was fun. Thrilling.

"I guess I get an adrenaline rush being on TV," she said softly.

"What exactly do you like about it?"

They were clearly gearing up for part two of the game they'd begun last night, testing the line that separated get-to-know-you politeness and…well, the sort of things you'd only do behind a closed door. He obviously wanted more than the taste of honey she'd been teasing him with while she'd eaten dinner and he'd watched.

And she wanted it, too. That was why she'd come here again. That was why she allowed her sweater to gape open, showing a bit more of her dress as she turned toward the mansion on the cliff.

Her pulse kicked, the oxygen thin in her lungs, making her voice breathy. "I've never told anyone this before."

"You can tell me."

What was it about him that made her expose a different side of herself?

"I like knowing that whoever is watching me on TV turned the channel so they could see me and what I do in the kitchen," she said. "I like that they *want* to watch." She took a step toward the mansion—just the first of hopefully many more. "I like wondering what they're thinking as they watch me."

Her heartbeat accelerated as she waited for his response.

When it came, his tone was rough. "What am I thinking right now?"

"You tell me."

"I'm sure you already know. You came back to this mansion tonight knowing."

Bolder and bolder. And with each passing second, throbs of hot blood took her over—in her chest, her belly, her clit.

Here it went.

"I think," she said, "that *you* liked the little show I put on for you with the food last night, and now you're watching how the wind is playing with my dress. You're wondering if I'm just a tease and I'm going to give you only a peek of leg before I reach down and smooth the material over my thighs so you don't catch an accidental look at what's underneath my skirt."

Even as she said it, the breeze was getting the best of the cotton, making it inch up. She fought the good-girl instinct to push the skirt down.

He spoke. "You're right. But I'm also hoping…"

"What?"

"That the wind is going to help me out and lift that skirt higher, even if you don't."

Ba-boom. His blunt words hit her with the force of a pounding wave, making her stomach swirl and her clit ache.

The decent Leigh—the one who'd grown up obeying all the rules and never coloring out of the lines— would've bolted now that she had nothing more to fulfill for the basket date. But the decent girl had already left the building, and a new girl had arrived.

"I've never objected to offering help when it's needed," Leigh whispered.

As the salty wind blew around her, silence reigned. She'd never done sassy come-ons before with a man. Sex for her had always been perfunctory. Short-term encounters without heat or heart. The only kind of sex that girls with shaky self-esteem had.

This was truly the line she and Callum had been tiptoeing around, and once she fully crossed it, there was no going back.

With a delicious quiver, she crossed it.

Her gaze locked on the brooding mansion as she clutched at her skirt with one hand, then slowly, painstakingly, purposely eased up the material. It slid up her thigh, whispering over her skin with sensuous deliberation.

Was his blood screaming through him just as sharply as hers? Was he also holding his breath, waiting? Needing?

When she got to the top of her thigh, she stopped.

"Red or white?" she said into the phone, unable to resist teasing him. "Devil or angel?"

New Leigh was good at this.

"Does it matter what color your underwear is?" he asked, sounding impatient.

"To me? Absolutely. Undies always matter to a girl, even if you guys don't care."

"I care." His laugh was jagged. "Show me which one you're wearing, Leigh."

She laughed. "You'll need to tell me something about yourself first. Like…do you really have black hair, or is that just what you told me last night to make yourself more mysterious?"

Now his laugh was really amused.

"I've got dark hair, just like millions of other men. Is that good enough for you?"

He didn't say anything more. But she was already looking around her to see that she was still alone on the beach and that there weren't any other mansions close enough to see what she was doing.

She coaxed her skirt up higher, showing him her delicate white panties.

"I had a feeling they'd be angelic," he said, and she could tell from his tone that the color *did* matter.

Behind her, the waves sounded as if they were coming in harder, and she felt the push and pull of them in her belly. Desire was washing through her, hot and getting more forceful by the second.

Finally, he spoke. "It's time for you to come inside, Leigh."

ADAM DIDN'T WAIT for her to climb up the wood steps that led to the rear of the mansion, where he'd left the back door by the pool unlocked for her.

He had already walked away from the darkened window on the top floor where he'd been standing, watching her on the beach. Watching as she'd revealed a small part of herself to him with such demure sensuality.

A peek of white panties.

The sight of underwear had never worked him up so much, making him go hard so quickly. And maybe it wasn't the lingerie itself that turned him on—it was the fact that he'd heard from Beth that Leigh wasn't a woman who slept around much. She also hadn't had any long-term relationships that Beth knew of, but there Leigh was on the beach, sexy as hell, pulling up her dress for him.

All he wanted to do right now was go downstairs to one of the living rooms, where he'd built a fire earlier, where he'd laid down blankets and oversize silk pillows along with the wine chilling in an ice bucket and the gourmet cheese plate he'd put together. And he wanted to see her face as he stepped into the room.

Would she recognize the quiet boy who'd left college after such a short time to become a man on his family's ranch?

Of course not. There was no way she would remember him—not from merely one party when he'd seen her across the room and hadn't even gone over to introduce himself. If he did show himself to her tonight, she would get a "who are you?" blankness in her eyes.

He felt a pang but brushed it off, telling himself that not being recognized by Leigh didn't matter. He just didn't want to destroy what they had going on—something nearly anonymous and definitely temporary.

He wouldn't even need to touch her to get his fill tonight. His heart couldn't take it, because after all this time, it still hadn't healed from Carla. It never would.

He headed straight for the darkened upper floor above the living room then reclined in the chair he'd placed behind the barred railing.

They had disconnected their call after he'd told her to take the stairs to the mansion, but now, as he heard the back door open and shut, he dialed her disposable cell, and she answered, out of breath.

He spoke before she could. "Take the hallway."

"You realize that if this were a horror movie, I'd be setting myself up as the girl who everyone in the audience yells at because she's walking into danger."

Again, her sense of humor. "This isn't a horror movie, and I'm not dangerous."

"Seriously? Because my friend Margot compared this whole setup to a scary story yesterday."

"But you're not scared."

"You're right. Besides, the hallway doesn't give off much of a sense of danger. It's dim, not dark."

The wall sconces were set on low, and he'd known it would be enough to light her way. "Are you at the end yet?"

"Near enough."

"Turn right."

He could almost feel her approaching—the ache inside of him got edgier with every thud of his pulse.

"Are you in the living room yet?" he asked.

"The one with the fire, blankets and Cleopatra spread? Yeah, I think so."

He was near enough that he could have raised his voice and she would've heard, but he didn't want to break the illusion that he wasn't quite there. It only added to the exhibitionist feel of this game, and she'd already admitted that she enjoyed being watched.

She appeared below him, the phone to her ear as she looked around at the Italian leather–upholstered furniture, the framed Renaissance sketches on the wall, the brass trimmings reflecting the flames from the fire. He swallowed. Hard.

Leigh took his breath away every time he saw her, and for a moment he wished he were a different man. Wished that he could click off the phone and go downstairs to touch her long blond hair or brush his fingers down her face, feeling her skin.

But he was the same old Adam—the guy Beth had accused of being abnormal last night. And that was all he would ever be after Carla.

He leaned his forearms on his thighs, his phone to his ear, watching through the upper-floor rails, totally shrouded in shadow. "Put your phone on speaker and lay it on those blankets."

"I guess your wish is my command." Smiling, she bent to a knee, placing the phone on the ground near a big gold-fringed pillow. "What now?"

He could hear his muffled voice coming through the phone on her blanket. "I'll leave what's next up to you."

His words seemed to ring through the air. It was up to her: stay or go. Advance or retreat.

Obviously, she hadn't expected this. He'd been giving the suggestions, unless you counted the time she'd demanded to know what color his hair was. But that had been a trivial thing, easily given up. A lot of men had dark hair and it wouldn't reveal much about him.

No fool, she glanced toward the upper floor, and his throat beat with his pulse just as if he'd been discovered. At the same time, she sat down on the blanket, slipping off her baggy white sweater, tossing it aside.

The fire crackled behind her, casting a golden glow over her as she reached for the wine in its bucket.

"A 2009 Riesling. Good pick, Callum."

"It goes well with the cheeses, especially the Parmigiano-Reggiano."

She plucked a slice off the silver tray, then fetched the lone wineglass, unstopped the cork and poured. "Are you drinking up there, too?"

"I was getting around to it." Glancing at the standing silver ice bucket with the same wine sticking out of it, he reached for a glass near his own chair, then poured. He lifted his drink in a toast even though she couldn't see him. "To fun and games."

"I'll drink to that."

She raised her glass, toasted him, then took a sip. When she was done, she nibbled on the cheese and put it down. Truthfully, she looked a little nervous as she scooted back against a large pillow facing him.

"Leigh," he said, "you know that this doesn't have to go any further. I don't want you to feel like I'm expecting anything."

She touched the hem of her dress, her long bare legs

stretched out in front of her, tipped by those hot cowgirl boots. "I wouldn't have come inside this mansion if I…" Her words trailed off until she added, "I've never given in to my whims all that much in life."

And she was determined to change that now?

His heartbeat seemed to be the only sound besides the crackle of flames in the fireplace.

Instead of talking, she held her wineglass in one hand, her other still touching the hem of her skirt. His cock pressed against the fly of his jeans, making him shift in his seat.

She lowered her voice, but he could still hear her loud and clear over the phone.

"What color are your eyes, Callum?" she asked, winding the material of her skirt around a finger, lifting it a touch higher.

So this was how it would go. Her asking questions, him giving in. Smart woman.

But he could play this.

"They're brown." He wouldn't tell her they were almost gold. For some reason it was too much detail, but brown was still close enough to the truth.

She laughed. "Funny. With a name like Callum, I pictured blue eyes."

"Because it sounds so Irish, huh?" He wouldn't tell her that he'd assumed his grandpa's name for this charade.

Instead of pulling up her skirt like last time, she instead reached up and idly rested her fingers at her collarbone, just above the buttons on her bodice. "Good. I can start putting together a real picture of you now that I know a couple of details."

It wouldn't be much of an image, and once again he

almost wished he could go to her, revealing himself so she could fantasize about him when this night was over, lying in bed, touching herself.

She was toying with the first button, and he waited to see where she was going to go with this. Waited as pressure built in his cock.

Unable to stand it, he said, "Why don't you just do it, Leigh?"

"Because you didn't say *please*." She'd lowered her gaze, looking up at him through her lashes like a temptress.

Damn it all. "Please."

Clearly noticing the edgy note in his tone, she undid the button. His lungs felt about ready to burn up.

Her smile grew, as if she were imagining him devouring her with his gaze. As if she were getting off on it just as much as he was.

She undid another button. Another.

When she was near the waistline, she stopped, her bodice gaping, showing him a lacy white bra that matched what he'd seen of her panties.

"White lace," he murmured.

She propped one of her booted feet on the blanket, leaning back on the pillow, giving him the sauciest look he'd seen from her yet while casually waving her knee back and forth. He could see a glimpse of her underwear, and it almost set something loose in him.

He was throbbing hard now, his cock straining from the steam whistling through his veins and gathering down below.

"Are you sure you don't want to come down here with me?" she asked.

His mouth was dry, and he swallowed again. "I think

you know the answer." Temporary. No name or face. No consequences.

"That's too bad. I'm having a lot of fun, even all by myself."

He was, too. More than he'd had since... God, he wasn't going to think about Carla.

Leigh reached for her wineglass, then lazily drank from it, putting it down again. Every move she made was innocently arousing, as if she had no idea that he was about to shoot through the roof. But from the way she kept slyly peeking up at him, he knew that she knew.

"If I'd had more wine already," she said, running a hand along the inside of one thigh, "I'd say that I feel a buzz. But I've only had a little, and…"

"What?" The word had scratched his throat.

She gave him one of those lowered-lash glances again. "I feel like I can do anything and not go home regretting it."

Her fingers came dangerously close to the juncture of her thighs, and he sucked in a sharp breath.

She laughed again, as though she was having the time of her life. "I feel even more reckless than last night because I know that what happens in this house…"

"Stays in this house."

No strings. Mystery dates that would stay mysterious because she didn't know who he was and never would.

As if wanting to prove what she'd just said, she bit her lip, then let her leg cant to the side, exposing more of her panties. But this time, she slid her hand to them.

He officially couldn't breathe now, couldn't move, either, for fear that he would break apart when he should be holding himself together. Yet as she coasted her fingers over herself, he couldn't take his eyes off her.

Leigh. The object of his youthful fantasies come to life right before him. But she was a wicked, confident woman now.

"What are you imagining?" he asked, pretending that her fingers were his.

"You."

He stifled a curse, then said, "Why don't you close your eyes. Keep picturing me."

Her long hair spread around her, one arm was crooked above her head in abandon. She was still biting her lip, her head turned to the side as she tentatively stroked herself.

He knew she was feeling shy even now. "I'm there with you, my fingers on you. How do they feel?"

"Nice," she whispered. "Really good."

He wanted more than good. "Slide your fingers into your panties, under that white lace. Touch yourself like you want me to touch you."

For a second he thought he might be rushing things, that she would realize how crazy this all was and put a stop to it. But then he heard a slight moaning sound over the phone as she obeyed, slipping her fingers into her underwear, arching her hips at the contact.

His dream girl, making fantasies into a reality right here, right now. Holding back his own moan, he imagined working her, making her wet.

"Now," he said, "take your other hand. Slip it inside your bra."

She did, and as her hips moved with the strokes of her fingers, her lips parted. She rubbed her breast slowly, just as he would've done if he'd been down there.

"Do you want me inside you?" he asked.

"Yes," she whispered.

Without any more instructions, she rocked her hips as she slid her fingers into herself.

He couldn't say anything else, could only fantasize about having his cock inside her, thrusting, his skin against hers. His mouth against hers, capturing the tiny cries of ecstasy that he was hearing now as she brought herself pleasure.

His cock was hard, demanding some private release, but he wanted to stay here, keep watching her, making himself wait, stretching out the sawing buzz of lust that was starting to pierce him through and through.

With every churn of her hips, every labored breath, he struggled to hold back, even while that steam rose in him, powering through his veins with cutting speed until—

She stifled a cry, then hitched in a quick breath, taking her hand out of her bodice and curling that arm over her face as if…as if she was hiding from him the way he was hidden from her.

He was gripping the armrest with one hand while she came, pressing her face into her arm.

When she was done, she panted, then started laughing. Now she was embarrassed?

"Well," she said. "Beth told me that our date would be fun. I can't say I've ever had so much fun in this way, though."

He laughed, too, but the sound was so tight that it barely came out. All he knew was that he'd have to have much more from Leigh than he'd gotten already.

And he had to figure out a way to touch her himself without unmasking "Callum."

5

As Leigh sat up, straightening her dress, her bodice still open, she thought, *Is this a good time to be mortified?*

Had this game gone a little too far?

Probably. But the thing was, she wasn't completely embarrassed about it. At first, maybe, but now it felt as if she'd just gotten off a breathtaking ride and her adrenaline was pumping away, telling her to get back on, to take another turn around the exhilarating track.

As if rebelling against all the deeply ingrained instincts that were trying to get her to use some common sense, she left the top of her dress open. See? She could be a desirable, sexy woman who made no apologies. She could revel in the aftermath of a seriously indulgent moment.

While she looked up at the top floor, her bra pushed up her breasts, making them rounded and sexy. Callum was probably still looking at them.

Freedom. This was truly freedom: knowing that your partner—or whatever he was—was gazing at you and not thinking you were overweight. Freedom was feeling high and ecstatic after that orgasm he'd given her with a bit of fantasy and the dark velvet sound of his voice.

Who'd ever made her feel that way before—and without even *being* here?

She smiled at the darkness where she knew he was sitting, though she could see only the brass railing in the firelight. Her vivid imagination made her think that she could also detect the outline of a man up there, reclining in a chair.

What would he do if she sprinted upstairs? Would he be gone before she got even halfway there?

She grabbed her wineglass, taking a long drink, then reached for the slice of cheese she'd started to eat before. When she was done with it, she said, "So, what's next on the agenda?"

Just listen to her, sounding as if she brazenly touched herself in front of hidden men every day of the week.

His deep, tight laugh made her nipples go hard again.

Narrowing her gaze, she said, "You don't actually have anything planned, do you?"

"Not true."

He sounded strained, and she took great delight in that because she'd gotten to him. She was in first place in this contest. *Finally.*

He continued. "I've got dinner warming in the oven. Just a simple shrimp linguine."

"Something you effortlessly whipped up?" With the wineglass in one hand, she plucked the phone off the blanket with the other, standing up, stretching. Teasing him a bit more with her body and reveling in it.

He cleared his throat. "I cook every so often, but I always need an easy recipe to work from. I'm not a good freestyler."

"Don't tell anyone, but I play it pretty safe in the kitchen. I know I do damned good comfort food—that's why people wanted me as their private chef—but it was my show's producers who added that flirty country presentation you see on TV. I've never been what you'd call avant-garde with my flavors." It was more comfortable that way, knowing where she was going, never deviating from what was tried and true.

Except for tonight.

She wandered toward the side of the room, where a stereo system waited behind the glass doors of a dark wood cabinet. She could tell Callum's gaze was tracking her, and the rush of desire that had overwhelmed her just minutes ago heated up again.

"Go ahead," he said as she peered at the setup. "Open it. There's an iPod dock in there, and you can choose what you want to hear from the playlists."

She did as he suggested, accessing the device, looking at the songs he had downloaded. "Lots of classic country, I see. You're a Johnny Cash fan?"

"Born and bred. Why don't you put one of his songs on?"

She randomly chose a title from the playlist, then listened to the guitar and echoing percussion, swaying a little to the beat. "I haven't heard Johnny Cash in years. I dated a guy once who..." She decided against dragging out the past, shaking her head. "Forget it."

"Tell me. You dated a guy once who did what?"

He actually sounded as if he wanted to hear about her boring romantic life up until now. Suddenly, a different sort of line appeared in front of Leigh, and this one wasn't about how far she would go on a strange date.

This one was more about how much of herself she was willing to give this man.

Was he into mind games just as much as the ones they were playing physically?

She'd find out. "It's on the tip of my tongue to say that I'm embarrassed to tell you about ex-boyfriends, but that would seem silly after..." She glanced back at the blanket and pillows. "Well, you know."

"I'm interested, Leigh. But you don't have to tell me anything you don't want to."

Again, he wasn't pushing her, and that made her more comfortable.

"He was my first boyfriend," she said, looking at the fire. "Although I'm not sure *boyfriend* is the right term."

"Why?"

"I think both of us were under some peer pressure to date. In senior year I hung out with a group of girls who all got serious boyfriends at the same time, leaving me the odd one out. He was buddies with one of my friends' best friends, and he was single, and...it just went from there. Movie nights with the crowd, school dances.... I was curious and he was curious, and the next thing I knew, it happened in the backseat of his car while we were parked on Glen Gulley Lane with a Johnny Cash cassette playing."

She didn't add that during their backseat fumblings, she hadn't felt much of anything. Just a teenage curiosity about sex, as well as a need to get it over with. She'd also tried her best to keep as many clothes on as possible, which hadn't been awkward *at all*. Right. It was just that she hadn't wanted him to see what she looked like with her clothes off.

"What happened afterward?" Callum asked. For

some reason, he sounded as if she'd been telling a sad story.

"We kept dating for a little bit longer," she said, refusing to let him believe her life was that pathetic. "For a month more, at least. Then it faded away like some high-school relationships do." And when he'd asked someone else to prom three months later, it hadn't bothered her.

Really. It hadn't. On that night, she'd had a fun time with a few friends at home, eating ice cream, chips and fast food in front of a scary-movie marathon on TV. It'd been about a week before Hannah had drowned, and after that the bingeing had just gotten worse.

Callum didn't say anything for a moment, but then his voice came back on the phone. "Letting you go was his loss."

She laughed. "Honestly, it was a long time ago, and it wasn't like he was the love of my life."

"Who was?"

She didn't have an answer, and that sounded even sadder than the story she'd just told.

"Let's just put it this way," she said, walking away from the stereo and toward the fire. "I've always been a free agent, and I like my status." She took a quick swig of wine before wrapping one arm over her chest as she stared into the flames.

"Good," he said simply.

"Good?"

"I don't believe in being tied down, either, anymore. Life's too short."

Anymore? What did that mean?

She started to turn around, seeing an opening to find out, but he cut her off.

"Don't think that you're going to get a story out of me, Leigh."

"Oh, come on, just one tiny anecdote? Something from high school, college? A disastrous-date story to amuse me?"

"I'm afraid that my stories aren't so amusing."

It was as if a knife had slashed the invisible screen between them, reminding her that this wasn't your average date, and he wasn't your average man.

And God help her, but that intrigued her more than ever.

She stared at the darkness above her, thinking that she saw some movement—a hand reaching up to push back some hair?

Then the image was gone.

Her heart jarred in her chest, but she calmed it, shaking her head and drinking more wine.

Then she lightly said into the phone, "Not knowing who you are is going to dog me, you know. Was that your intention? To frustrate the hell out of me even after this date?"

"Never." The word was loaded, as if he'd just made some sort of decision. He sounded distant for some reason. "I don't intend to frustrate you."

"I'm only joking with you, Callum, but I have to wonder.... I'm not sure there's anywhere to go from, well, what we just did." A more immediate version of phone sex. "I doubt there's much mileage in only watching me all night."

"I could watch you for…" He stopped.

What had he been about to say? He could watch her for hours? Days? Why did she think that he might've even been about to say "forever"?

That was ridiculous, though. He didn't know her and she didn't know him, at least not well enough so that she could guess his identity from his voice or his taste in rental mansions. The only interest he had in her was for one or two dates.

Even so, her stomach fell a bit at the thought that this would be over soon.

She listened to the music a little longer, and when she glanced back up at the railing, she could've sworn that he wasn't there anymore. She didn't know why; she just felt it.

"Why don't you come to the dining room?" he said over the phone.

Yup, he'd left the upper floor, because now that she was paying more attention, she couldn't hear that faint echo of his real voice anymore. It was all phone.

She made her way out of the room, going to the long table set with bone china, a bottle of chilled French Chardonnay by her plate beside a corkscrew. A warmed bowl of his shrimp linguine awaited, along with a salad that he must've stored in the refrigerator.

So he *had* sneaked off at some point, and he'd done it because he wanted to put the food on the table.

"Damn," she said as she sat in the same chair that she had last night. "Seems I just missed you."

"Seems you did." He sounded pumped, as if the risk of being caught had turned him on.

He didn't have to tell her to help herself to the offerings. She knew the drill by now.

And she wished this wouldn't be the last strange date with the man who'd somehow become more than a basket date to her.

WHEN LEIGH OPENED the door to the hotel room she was sharing with Margot, her friend hopped out of her bed, pushing her computer from her lap and throwing off her covers.

She didn't even have to ask—she just gave Leigh a wide-eyed look.

"You totally did it with him," she said. "Oh, my God, Leigh. You had sex with the Phantom!"

Leigh almost gave in to the urge to lead Margot on just for the fun of it but didn't. "There was no sex involved. Not the regular kind anyway."

"What?"

It was pretty satisfactory when Leigh meandered toward the bathroom and Margot chased her down. There'd been so many times in the past when the tables had been turned, and now who had the exciting life?

Actually, life had been exciting up until the moment she had walked out Callum's door and gotten into the waiting limo. She hadn't been expecting any miracles tonight, like seeing him step out of the shadows to reveal his identity, but she'd at least wanted…

What? A meaningful connection with a man who'd never asked her for more than fun and games?

"Leigh, you'd better answer me," Margot said, pulling up behind her as Leigh flipped on the bathroom light. "Do you know what I've been doing this whole time? Making last-minute arrangements for Dani's surprise wedding party get-together next week at the ranch." A bunch of sorority sisters were gathering to work on reception plans, unbeknownst to Dani. Any excuse for a party. "Oh," Margot added, "I almost forgot that I was *also* obsessing about what was happening on your second date. Spill! What do you mean that you kind of had sex with him?"

Leigh shrugged, grinning as she rested her phone on the counter and then fetched an elastic band out of her beauty bag, whipping her hair off her shoulders and into the kind of no-fuss do she normally wore. Then, still taxing Margot's patience, she walked toward the tub, running the water and adding the sweet-smelling gel the hotel had provided.

"Excuse me?" Margot said.

"I'm just taking a bath. I've never really put aside time to do that, you know? But I'm in the mood to be a Calgon girl." She wanted to relax, have some alone time, think about Callum. She was still worked up, damn it. Unfulfilled.

"So that's it?" Margot threw up her hands, cuffing the sides of her button-down nightshirt in the process. "You're going radio silent on me?"

Leigh began to unbutton her sweater, and Margot gave a frustrated sound, then walked out, half shutting the door behind her, just like in college when they'd roomed together. God knew how many bathroom chats they'd had while one of them would shower and the other one would put on makeup or fix her hair just outside the door. Margot had never minded stripping down in front of others, but Leigh? She'd never dared.

Times, they had a-changed. Thinking of how far she'd gone tonight, Leigh took off her clothes while Margot said, "Okay. I get it. You're punishing me for keeping the whole book contract thing to myself, and because I didn't tell you about my fling with Clint right away."

"No, I'm not." She turned off the water, then got into

the tub. The bubbles surrounded her, tickling her chin as she sank into luxury.

"Then you just want to keep everything to yourself. I understand."

Maybe she'd tortured Margot enough. "Just come in here, Marg."

Margot hesitated. And why not, when Leigh had never allowed anyone to get within range whenever she was undressed?

Her friend crept into the bathroom and sat on the closed toilet seat, giving Leigh the raised eyebrow. Was she wondering what was up with the newfound "you can be in here when I'm nekid" attitude?

Negligently flicking some bubbles with her thumb and index finger, Leigh grinned. "I've never met anyone like him. He knew just what to say to me." How to make the woman come out in her, and how to make her touch herself in all the right places.

"Did he reveal his identity?"

"No."

"But you kind of had sex with him."

"Sort of?"

"Leigh, you're driving me ding-dong here."

"All right, we'll start from the beginning. Let's just say that after I got to his place, I took a walk on the deserted beach and talked with him on a phone he gave me."

Margot crossed her arms over her chest. "And that's when he said 'all the right words' to you. He sweet-talked you the whole night?"

"I'd say so." Leigh submerged herself to just below her mouth, sliding an impish glance to Margot. "I had the equivalent of phone sex with him."

"On the beach?"

Leigh only smiled as Margot's eyes slowly got wider than she'd ever seen them, even after that night in college when Leigh had downed five Killer Kamikaze shots and still been able to walk a straight line at their main hangout, Desperado's.

"You had pseudosex on the beach," Margot repeated.

"I only flashed my undies at him there. But once we were inside, things went a little further."

"Oh, God, I don't want to ask how far." Margot covered her face, then uncovered it. "Okay, how far?"

A rascally smile was the only answer Leigh gave.

"That far," Margot said, breaking into a reluctant grin. "You devil, you. I didn't know you had it in you. Did anything else happen after that?"

"Sure. I ate alone again and we had a good chat about movies and books. Turns out he likes thrillers."

Margot was still waiting, and when she clearly realized that Leigh had nothing more to offer, she stood. "So you weren't lying. There was no sex with you two from that point on."

"Not even another raunchy phone call." And that had confused her more than anything. It'd been as if, after she'd teased him about being frustrated, he'd decided that he'd pushed her far enough and had acted the gentleman the rest of the night.

"Then you left his house?" Margot asked. "With just a fond goodbye?"

"Right. And you know what? I don't regret a minute of what did happen. I had a great time, and I found out some things about myself. I never thought I'd be the type of woman who'd…you know."

"Get off in front of a guy you don't know?"

"Yeah, that." It sounded so dirty. So *fun*. "But I am that girl, Marg. And I loved being her."

"Wow." Margot pushed back a dark wave that had escaped from her ponytail. "I mean, *wow*. The Leigh I used to know wouldn't have gone on that date, first of all. And second, she wouldn't have been a wanton lady like you were. She would've been too bashful."

"It crossed my mind to be weirded out by what I'd done, but I wasn't. This sounds strange, but even though I don't know him, it seemed like I did, right off the bat. I've never been so in tune with anyone in my life."

"Do you think you do know him, and that's why he's familiar?"

"I hope not." She smoothed her hand over the bubbles. "That would change everything. It would make things…"

"Serious. I understand. But this way you can go about your business without there being any consequences."

"Exactly." She sighed. "All I was looking for was adventure. But I got more than that."

"You sure did."

"No, that's not what I mean. Now I'm wondering what I've been missing my entire life by being so cautious. By staying in that shell I built because I was chubby and unattractive."

Margot raised a finger. "You were always pretty, Leigh. I wish you wouldn't say that."

"Don't blow sunshine at me. I was always the one with the good personality and you know it."

"You still do have the good personality."

As Margot smiled down at her, a dinging sound from outside interrupted them.

"Your phone," Margot said, and there was a brightness in her eyes.

Before Leigh could say anything, Margot had jetted out of the bathroom and returned with the phone in hand, peering at the screen.

"Squee-mail," she said, smiling like a maniac.

As Margot showed her the screen, Leigh saw that there definitely was reason to squee.

It was a message from Beth Dahrling, and all it said was "He's got a proposition for you."

ADAM HOVERED OVER Beth's shoulder as she sent the email from her smartphone in his kitchen.

She glanced behind her, irritation written all over her exotic features, and Adam backed off, raising his hands.

"Sorry," he said, grinning.

"It's not like she's going to answer with light speed." She put the phone on a marble counter and turned to him. "She might even be in bed by now. And speaking of bed, I'm off to mine. I'll leave my phone here so you can pretend to be me or…whatever."

She started to abandon him, her long silk skirt swishing behind her, leaving a trace of jasmine perfume. His assistant had been hanging out at the nearby bar in the fancy hotel down by the shore-lined Highway 101, just as she'd been doing every night since they'd gotten here.

It was a lonely job working for a hermit like him, he realized. Not much opportunity to meet anyone—not even if you were a looker like Beth.

"Wait," he said. "You're not up for a cocktail? This is our last night here, so why not enjoy it while we can?"

"Because I've got to pack."

"Beth."

She rolled her eyes, gesturing toward the liquor cabinet, which had everything from vintage Scotch to sweet Amaretto. He'd stocked every minibar in the mansion the same way when he'd arrived.

Getting out two cut-crystal glasses from the cupboard, he chose the Amaretto, then used ice from the refrigerator before he poured the liquor over the cubes.

He handed a glass to Beth. "Here's to a few days in the country."

"Really? You want me to drink to that?"

"Why not?"

"Because you're not really going home yet. When we first came here, your plan was to have this date and that was it. Now you ask me to make late-night arrangements for your 'get away from it all' ranch to be opened up so you can invite Leigh there and continue this madness. I've got to be a sucker to please you."

Adam swirled the liquor in his glass. That "get away from it all" place she was referring to was a small spread in the San Pasqual area of San Diego that he'd bought after Carla's death. It was a gentleman's operation with a stable of a few horses and a small vineyard. Not that this ranch allowed him to get away from the computer, where he did most of his business investing, managing his healthy stock portfolios. He also had to keep up with his research so he could acquire more resort properties and biotech businesses to keep him in the flush. But it was nice to have the option to get away, especially when memories of Carla got to be too much for him in the places they'd been together.

"I won't be there for long," he said. "And you get to go home. But it all depends on Leigh and her answer. She's on hiatus for her show, and I don't have to be physically present at any meetings to please any business boards for about a week, so it's a good time for both of us."

"You sure made it sound that way in the email. 'How about a few days away from it all?'" she quoted. "'Callum wants you to join him for a few more games next week as his guest.'"

The idea had evolved throughout the evening and had come to a lightbulb moment after Leigh had mentioned being frustrated when their date was over. She'd also said that she didn't know how far they could take this watching game, and he'd wondered if she was already tired of it.

So he'd decided to back off at that point, hoping that withholding sexual games would make her long for more. Then he'd sprung this invitation on her. All that remained was her answer.

"I'll make all the time and effort you've spent on this up to you," he said to Beth. "In fact, you might want to check your email account as soon as I get on my computer and forward you the information. There should be a message about an online shopping spree through your favorite designer boutiques…."

"Bribery." She seemed angry, but then she gave him a tolerant, affectionate glare that only someone like a big sister could get away with.

"It comes close," he said, smiling back. "Besides, this is just one last hurrah with Leigh, and then I'm letting this go. Promise."

"Is that what you were thinking during your romantic night together? That you only want one more hurrah?"

"Of course."

"Sure." She put down her untouched drink. "Now, I don't know what went on between the two of you tonight, but I saw the pillows and blanket in front of the fire. And it looked like someone had been using them."

He sighed. "I know where you stand on this. You don't want her hurt. Or me."

"It's you I'm worried about the most at this point."

He frowned.

"You know exactly what I mean," she said. "Last night was only one date. But now you've started to really like Leigh, and it's only a matter of time before you start feeling guilty about betraying Carla with another woman. I've seen you get intrigued by a couple of your so-called pen pals on the internet, and it's always the same—when you start getting interested, you start getting dark and angry at life because it took the only woman you've ever loved away from you, and you decide you're not going to let it happen again. That's when you go into major seclusion."

He gripped his glass. She was right. He didn't like to get too close, because every time he did, he saw Carla in his mind's eye.

On her deathbed, he'd vowed to her that she'd be the only one, ever, even though she'd never made him promise it. And even if he needed his libido perked up every so often, he intended to keep his vow to the woman he'd loved heart and soul.

"Leigh's not expecting anything to happen between us," he finally said. "Neither am I. I've told you that. A few more days won't matter."

"You're already fighting tooth and nail to pretend you're not falling heart-first into this, Adam. Every word you're saying is empty."

Just as empty as he felt most of the time? But *hadn't* there been a few moments tonight when he'd felt something? Because when Leigh had told him about her first real boyfriend, his chest had folded inward. And watching her pretend that the story hadn't mattered had been all the sadder.

Yet that was the point, wasn't it? Leigh hadn't made a big deal about anything emotional. She definitely knew how to keep her sadness at bay, and he needed that, at least for a short time more. Both of them could cut this brief affair off before it meant anything.

"If Leigh says yes to this," he said, "she would know that this extended date would be the last. You don't need to worry about either of us, Beth."

"No worries. Got it."

She seemed extra sensitive tonight, and he reached out his free hand, touching her arm.

"You okay?" he asked.

"Definitely." She let out a sigh, obviously knowing it was useless to lie to him. "At the bar, I finally decided to go ahead and join a nunnery because I'm so tired. Tired of looking, tired of trying, tired of talking to a woman and realizing that there's no connection there. Do nunneries still exist?"

"I have no idea."

He squeezed, and she smiled faintly. Two of a kind. No wonder they'd ended up together.

A ding on her phone brought them out of their silence, and he didn't move. Was it Leigh?

Beth grabbed the phone and accessed the screen.

"And…?" Adam asked.

"She says, 'What do you have in mind, Callum?' I like how she doesn't beat around the bush and she answered you right away. Most women like to play games."

Most men did, too. Or maybe it was just him, with all these games he was playing with Leigh.

"Why *would* she hide her interest?" he asked.

"Yes," Beth said, arching a brow. "Why hide, *Callum?*"

He shot her a glare, and she held up the phone.

"Your answer?" she asked.

He smiled, taking the device from her, assuming Beth's identity while typing out the rest of his invitation.

And also assuming that Leigh was going to say yes to an offer no woman could refuse.

6

IT WAS DATE night for Dani and Riley, and after they came out of the movie theater, where they'd seen a late showing of an action movie he'd been pining for, they stopped by a coffee nook that was still open.

Dani told him that she'd get the beverages, and when she returned to their small mosaic-tiled table in a corner near a shelf of old leather-bound books and a fern plant, she slid their tray toward him, smiling.

"Coffee, tea…me?" she said, sitting down.

"She brings offers I can't refuse." He took his house-blend coffee, leaning back in his chair, propping his booted ankle on a jeans-clad knee.

Although he'd taken the coffee, Dani was sure he was talking about the "me" part, too; he was grinning at her with one of those intimate grins that assured her of his devotion, but a niggle still got to her.

Last night, when she'd brought out those blue fuzzy handcuffs and they'd played the "mysterious man" game inspired by Leigh's basket date, the sex had been amazing. But for some reason she couldn't put her finger on, she felt a distance from Riley, even if he was as affable as ever.

Was it because she'd sensed more frustration in him due to this experimental phase she was in? He hadn't exactly mentioned her having cold feet about the wedding, but...

She couldn't form any more thoughts after realizing how time was marching along and the ceremony was getting ever closer. Her skin seemed to jump with nerves.

Why, though? Riley was the love of her life. Yet how many people, like her divorced parents, had thought the same thing when they started out?

"Did you like the movie?" he asked.

"It was great. A total good time."

"I get the feeling you need a distraction more than usual. Besides your regular job, you've been burying yourself in planning for your catering company, not to mention the wedding stuff with Margot and Leigh."

"They want to do a lot of the wedding planning." Thank goodness. "Besides, it's my *future* catering company, and the workload now is nothing compared to what I'll be doing if I get that business loan."

"You will."

He seemed so confident about that, and she couldn't resist mirroring his grin.

They sipped their beverages, but her chai tea needed some cooling, so she blew on it. Meanwhile, silence came between them. It'd been there ever since last night when she realized she didn't know what to say to Riley when the fuzzy handcuffs and the blindfold had been packed in a kitchen drawer. But one thing that she hadn't been able to put away was the feeling that she'd gotten from those cuffs around her wrists, the shortness of breath that the light bondage had caused.

You need to think about who you really want, Dani, Riley had told her in the midst of their foreplay, when he'd been pretending to be the mystery man. His words had stayed with her even afterward, during a meal in which they didn't talk about the intense encounter they'd just had. The reality was that she felt more skittish than ever about the wedding.

Riley put his paper coffee cup on the table, clearly choosing his words before he ran a hand through his black hair and said, "You know that there's an elephant in this room, and it's sitting right on our table."

She wasn't going to play dumb. She glanced around the shop, but they were the last customers and the employees were cleaning behind the counter, getting ready to close. Serene world music played over the speakers, masking their conversation.

"You're right about an elephant," she said. "I feel like I need to apologize for last night."

"No apologies necessary."

"You keep saying that, no matter how many times I put you through the wringer. It's one of the reasons I love you—because you've got the patience of a saint." Not for the first time, she wondered how long that patience was going to last.

Was she pushing him in that area just to see how much he would take? Would she be happy only when he did leave and validated her fears about broken marriages?

"Last night it wasn't patience you wanted from me," he said.

She leaned forward, setting her tea down, wrapping

her hands around the cup. A strand of her bobbed hair fell forward but she didn't tuck it back. Last night she hadn't known what she wanted out of Riley. Right now, though, sitting across from him, she couldn't imagine life without him. Her heart felt torn just thinking about it.

"Honestly, I don't know what I'm doing," she said. "I asked you to stick with me while we tried new things. New 'adventures' like Margot and Leigh were having." Sexual and career changes, just to see if they would change her. He kept saying that he was falling in love with her all over again while seeing this side of her.

"I'm always up for something new," he said. "But every day, I feel you getting a little further from me, Dani." He reached across the table and held her hand. "There're some demons you're trying to chase off, and I have to wonder if most of it's because of what your dad did...."

"If you don't mind, it'd be great if we didn't have to talk about him."

Riley held tight to her, his voice steady. "I'm not him."

She looked into Riley's blue eyes, nearly drowning in them, making her feel instead of think. One of those demons that nagged at her said, *Too many people in love don't think, and that's why they don't stay together.*

She held Riley's hand tightly. "Could you tell me the truth? Did you like it last night?"

Glancing at the employees behind the counter, he returned his gaze to her. "Dani, you could walk into a room in a sweat suit and that would work me up. We don't need toys or scenarios. We never did."

He'll get bored within a year if you don't spice it up

and keep his attention, said that ugly voice. *Just ask your dad....*

She reached over to smooth his hair back from his face. She didn't have to say that he really was enough for her; they'd been together for so long—engaged forever, it seemed—that they had their own ways of communicating.

It was also obvious, though, that Riley believed she was only going through a phase, that soon she'd stop bringing home exotic massage oils and toys from the naughty shops and go back to "normal."

She wasn't sure what that even meant anymore.

In a none-too-subtle hint that the coffee shop was closing, the lights dimmed.

Riley chuckled, leaning over to kiss her on the temple. "That's my cue to see a man about a horse. Be right back?"

Before he got up, she rashly angled over to press her lips to his. Bursts of color danced on the back of her eyelids, bright spots she couldn't hold on to, so she gripped him even closer.

When they were done, he took a breath. She'd caught him off guard, but he didn't mind.

She smiled at him as he stood, then walked off, leaving her alone.

After sending a "really, we're almost out of here" grin to the lingering employees, Dani got out of her seat. She left a tip and cleared the table, then strolled toward the door. She'd forgotten to turn her phone back on after the movie. As soon as it powered up, the screen showed her a voice-mail message she'd missed.

Margot.

Earlier, before the second mystery date, she and

Leigh had told Dani that they would call in the morning, so the fact that there was a change in plans worried Dani a bit, and she accessed the message.

"I swear, Leigh's gone off the deep end." Margot was whispering excitedly. "She's in the bath right now, la-di-daing away in there, so I'm sneaking in a call before tomorrow. Mystery Man invited her on a retreat for a few days next week. I know! And she's going, even though he still hasn't told her who he is."

A niggle haunted Dani again, but she tried to chase away the fear that if she didn't do something just as exciting with Riley, she was going to bore him all too soon.

And if he ever left? She'd be as devastated as she'd been when her parents had sat her down five years ago and told her that they weren't in love anymore.

The message continued. "We'll call you tomorrow morning, okay? Leigh can tell you all about how she was… To put it mildly, Dan, we're dealing with quite the advanced flirt, and I don't know where she came from. Leigh's definitely feeling her oats these days. You'll see. Anyway, I also wanted to tell you that Clint and I are really looking forward to your visit to the ranch next weekend—"

Dani stopped the message just as Riley was making his way toward her, and she tucked the phone into her purse.

They walked out of the shop, and he put his arm around her shoulders. Warm, safe, secure…. She wrapped her arms around his waist as they strolled in the direction of his truck.

"You ready for our little trip next weekend?" she asked.

"Wouldn't miss a jaunt over to Clint's." He was smiling, and she got the feeling he'd already talked to Clint about their plans. Or maybe he was smiling about something else, because he slipped his hand under her tight sweater, his fingertips touching her waist, sending a shiver through her.

"There're other trips I'd like to take you on first," he said.

"You can take me anywhere you want."

Later that night, he did, and she fell asleep in his arms before she could think about how much longer he'd be satisfied with this life.

LEIGH HAD NEVER experienced a longer stretch of time than the few nights she'd just gone through while waiting for Basket Date, Part Three.

When the day of departure came, a limo arrived at her home to take her to a small airport in Lodi where a private plane was waiting for her, stocked with champagne and hors d'oeuvres. She hadn't been told anything about this date but the basics, and she shivered a little anticipating the mysteries in store.

After they landed at McClellan-Palomar Airport in San Diego County, another limo showed up, with an elderly driver who asked her very politely to put on a blindfold.

A little embarrassed—and pretty turned on, too— she did so. The driver didn't even act as if this was an out-of-the-ordinary request for Callum to have made of her, and she figured that either her Mystery Man did this often with women or the driver worked for other kinky men besides Callum. Whatever, he seemed to take the quirks of his job in stride.

It was only after the longish drive, when the limo

had come to a stop, that she was allowed to remove the blindfold. As she got out of the car, she blinked, looking around her.

They were in the sunny countryside where it was quiet, and the driveway leading up to this hilltop was oak lined. A road wound by beneath the property, with wood fences paralleling the blacktop and horses wandering alongside in corrals. Orange trees surrounded them, and when she turned around, she saw the house: a Tuscan-style stone building that was big but wasn't quite a mansion, either. In the background she caught sight of the stables and, on the other side of the property, rows of grapevines.

"What do you have in mind this time, Callum?" Leigh asked herself as the driver went to fetch her luggage.

She wandered closer to a walkway with rosebushes on both sides. The scent of hay, flowers, oranges and fresh air revived her. She'd grown up on a ranch with horses, a modest converted farmhouse and a swimming hole that…

No, she wasn't going to think about the swimming hole, since that was where Hannah had died. But everything else about the country revived her, bringing to mind lazy days of summer when she would ride horse trails and cruise in pickups down the windy bucolic lanes because teens like her didn't have anything better to do.

The door to the house loomed just ahead of her, and Leigh hesitated on the walkway. Had this been a bad idea, accepting Callum's invitation to extend their date a few more days? She hadn't been able to resist the lure of maybe discovering who he was. And she was really curious about how they would interact if he insisted on keeping his identity a secret.

What kind of erotic games did he have planned? she also kept asking herself, and the possibilities had owned her.

Now she really knew what the phrase "Curiosity killed the cat" meant, she thought as she started walking again, approaching the doorway. But frankly, curiosity would've eaten her alive if she hadn't come here.

Earlier the driver had given her a disposable phone, and she'd been waiting for it to ring the entire time. It did just before she got to the door.

She answered it, looking up at the windows. Was he watching her arrive from one of them?

"How was your trip?" he asked in that smooth, caressing voice.

"Great."

"Good to hear. The door's unlocked."

Leigh guessed that was an invitation to stroll right in, so she obliged him. At the same time, she absently ran a hand over her hair, suddenly wishing she'd fixed it into something other than a low, very Leigh-like boring braid. Maybe she also should've worn something other than a simple white blouse that tied at the waist, a burgundy wraparound skirt and cowboy boots. But she hadn't known what Callum had in mind. How could she dress for the unexpected?

As she walked into the foyer, she took in the smooth stone floor and rustic wood furniture, along with a huge iron light fixture that reigned over the stairway. Italian country, Leigh thought, wondering how this reflected Callum's tastes.

"So this is your place?" Leigh asked.

"It actually belongs to...a friend."

Damn, thwarted again. But naturally, Callum would avoid having her stay at any property that gave even the slightest clue about him.

When the driver entered behind her, he headed toward the staircase.

"You travel light," Callum said as she followed the man.

So he *had* seen her through a window. Those erotic shivers consumed her again. "This is more baggage than I usually bring. I've learned to pack like a pro with all the traveling I do for the show, but I figured I'd need a few extras for this trip." Like several sets of the nicest lingerie she'd recently bought.

She saw the driver take a left down the hallway as Callum said, "So what did you bring here that you usually don't need for your show, Leigh?"

"A girl never tells." She wanted to save the lingerie for later.

For the newest scenario with Callum.

The driver had entered the second room on the right, and she walked in after he set her bags on her bed. Nodding to her, he left. Clearly, he'd been instructed to stay mum. But she didn't have time to dwell on that thought when she got a load of the elegant room. A white duvet-covered bed with embroidered throw pillows dominated the space. A bay window overlooked the small vineyard, and heavy damask curtains framed the glass. A massive cherrywood desk took over one corner while a case with delicate wrought-iron sculptures of leafless trees owned another. There was also a roomy armoire, plus dressers and nightstands, and a dressing screen decorated with images of the sun.

"Not a bad place to spend a few days in," Leigh said.

"Make yourself at home."

There was a note of pride in his voice, and it tweaked Leigh's curiosity. Walking into the bathroom, she almost sighed in pure delight. Marble floors and counters, a garden tub with a nearby shower, a light-studded vanity mirror connected to a table with a chair in front of it…. She already felt like royalty.

"This has got to be heaven," Leigh said into the phone.

"We haven't even gotten started." He paused. "Is there anything you need right now?"

She had a million requests that she knew he wouldn't fulfill…yet. "I don't know. Maybe a tiara?"

Laughing softly, he said, "There's a hot tub in the back, if you're interested, as well as a spa room and stables."

"Anything you don't have here?"

She could tell he was grinning. "I even thought about you and your cooking. I'm not going to put you to work or anything, but if you want to experiment in the kitchen with some state-of-the-art equipment, it's all yours, just like at the other mansion. But this one's even better stocked."

"With what?"

"Some experimental equipment, like appliances you'd use for molecular gastronomy dishes."

Leigh laughed. "I'm just a down-home cook who spices up her food with candlelight and innuendo. I haven't flirted a lot with food science."

"Be that as it may, this place is also outfitted with a multiunit range with gas burners, a wok burner, a griddle and a steamer or fryer. They're all at your disposal, but if you want to be waited on, there's staff available when you pick up the house phone."

"Will I be seeing any of them?"

"I've left instructions for us to be left alone as much as possible."

Alone. With Callum. Her breathing quickened.

"About the hot tub…" she said softly.

He waited, and she smiled.

"What if I didn't bring a bathing suit?"

He laughed again, but this time there was an aching darkness to it. Those shivers ran up and down and in and out. He sure knew how to make her want more of him.

"I should give you a chance to settle in," he said, and at the thought of him going, she resisted.

"I'm already settled," she said, exploring the room again, running her fingers over the clearly expensive dresser. "So…" She needed to talk; she didn't want him to go. "This is what it's like after you make it in life, huh?"

"What do you mean? You have a show on TV."

"It's not a blazing hit or anything, just a minor one." Enough to have allowed her to buy a ranch house as well as one for her parents, who'd retired twenty miles away from her.

She'd never thought that she was the type to yearn for riches, and maybe she wasn't. If anything, she was merely impressed by what she saw right now, but she didn't mind being treated as if she was valued every once in a while. Didn't mind it a bit.

"Is it so hard to admit that you're a success?" he asked.

His voice…. How had she come to be so attached to it? When would she get enough of it?

"I suppose I'm just modest," she said, not wanting to talk about always being in second place, always being the one who wasn't treated as well as Callum was treating her. She changed the subject. "Tell me, how many houses do you have?"

"Back to Twenty Questions, I see."

"I didn't want to disappoint you by changing my style. What else did you expect?"

"I expect that you'll be pampered to within an inch of your life the next few days. Everything you want, you'll get. Within reason, that is."

Ah, he knew her well, because the first thing she would've requested was answers. "I'm good with what I see so far."

He really was bent on spoiling her. But a tiny voice inside her started saying annoying things. *You know that he wouldn't be paying half as much attention to you if you were still chubby, right? Do you think he'd be as interested in you if you gained all that weight back?*

But he'd told her that she'd always been pretty, which meant that he'd seen her in her "heftier" days.

Yet the voice inside her could get so loud. Overwhelming. She needed to ignore it.

"Leigh," he said over the phone, and she blinked, coming back to the present.

"Yes?"

"Since you're settled, indulge me by stepping into the hallway."

So the games would start right away? Wasn't that how they functioned, though? Wasn't that all there was between them really?

Her blood started to pump with jerks of desire as she went to the door, opened it and walked into the hallway. Iron lanterns were posted on the walls, giving off dim light.

"Check the door on the left side at the end," he said.

When she got there, she opened the door and found it led to another bedroom, this one decorated in burnished tones with mosquito netting around the bed, hiding the mattress. This room had a view of the pool, which was shaped like a lagoon. A rock waterfall splashed into it.

He spoke again. "Open the armoire."

The hinges moaned softly as she obeyed, and she reached out to touch one of the beautiful pieces of clothing hanging there.

It was a flowing, sheer creation in a color that matched her dark green eyes, and it reminded her of something a woman would wear in a harem.

"What's this?" she asked.

"Only one of many choices."

She thought she heard something coming from an adjoining room, a shifting sound. Was Callum behind the door?

Don't go over to open it, she thought. *It'll only be locked, and you'll ruin what you have with him. Just be happy with this.*

But wasn't that what she wanted? The truth of who he was? Or were the games they were playing still too much of a rush to give up?

She went with the latter possibility for now, fingering another outfit—a silk suit that looked as though it belonged to a mobster. Gray pin-striped pants, a vest, a fine long-sleeved shirt, a fedora....

Her excitement went up another notch. She'd never dreamed of scenarios like the ones these clothes were suggesting. Well, okay, yes, she had dreamed of them, but to have them here at her fingertips?

"Go to the bed," he said.

Deserting the armoire, she followed his suggestion, turning her back on the door leading to the adjoining room. She pushed aside the hanging net and found more treasures on the mattress that the thin material had been hiding.

The first thing she saw was a flat, open white box, tissue spread out with yet another outfit draped over it.

A short negligee dress—creamy-white, filmy, one piece, no panties. But it did have a matching robe and thigh-high stockings. And there was one more item that made everything a little more erotic—ballet shoes. The kind that real dancers wore when they danced on their toes.

"I'm not a ballerina," she said, reaching out to brush the stockings. God, these were real silk. He'd gotten her the best.

"You don't have to dance for me, Leigh. You can just sit in a chair by the window with those shoes and the negligee on, looking like a satin doll." He paused. "What else do you see on that bed?"

She was utterly focused on discovering everything he'd laid out for her, completely steeped in this new set of fantasies.

As her gaze traveled to the right, she sucked in a breath, not quite knowing why these items were there.

Silken cords.... Feathers....

Before she could speak into the phone, she felt a length of silk slipping over her eyes, her sight blocked by the material.

She dropped the phone, reaching up in shock, her hands closing around a pair of wrists.

His wrists?

"Are you ready to start?" Callum's voice asked from right behind her.

7

As Leigh grasped his wrists, Adam loosened his hold on the blindfold.

"I'll stop if you want me to," he whispered.

She didn't say anything for a moment, and his pulse chopped through him so forcefully that he almost couldn't hear anything but his own heartbeat, his throttled breathing.

The scent of her hair...it was like strawberry fields. He hadn't ever guessed she'd smell like that, although it made perfect sense, wrapping her innocence and ripeness all into one. And as her fingers burned into his skin, he almost melted.

This close...yet this far from her.

"Is that you?" she asked. "Really you?"

"You'd better hope so." He waited. "Last time, you said you didn't know how far we could take the watching, so—"

"You're changing it up."

A wavering laugh came from her, and she let go of his wrists even as she kept her hands nearby, still raised in the air, as if she didn't know how else to react.

"I didn't think you'd do something like this," she said. "Aren't you afraid I'll take off the blindfold and turn around to see you?"

"No." Because then this would all become too real for both of them. "This way we don't owe each other anything. You go back to your life, I go back to mine, both of us remembering the single week we had with a fantasy."

She'd started to lower her hands all the way.

He kept whispering. "Part of me can't believe that you accepted this invitation. Then again, part of me knew that you would."

"Based on what I've seen so far, I would've been insane to refuse everything you have to offer."

God, her hair. He closed his eyes, taking in the scent, heady with it.

"Do you trust me?" he asked.

"To do what?"

"I'm not going to tell you, and that's why you have to trust me." All there would be in this so-called relationship was a tenuous thread—trust—joining their fantasies together. No emotion. Just two people who were happy with having each other's bodies.

Carla couldn't have faulted him for that. But when it came to his heart and giving it away to someone else? Never.

A few beats passed, stilted, as soft as a ticking watch pressed under a wad of cotton.

"I trust you," she said, lowering her hands all the way.

Something in his chest seemed to flip-flop, but he shoved that aside. She'd just given him permission to go ahead, and that was all he'd been hoping for.

He tied the blindfold at the back of her head. When he was done, he asked, "How does that feel?"

"Fine." He could tell she was off-balance by the way she took a tiny step to the side.

Instinctively, he laid his hands on her shoulders, feeling warmth beneath her blouse. Skin. Her.

His belly tumbled, his blood boiled.

"You sound—" she seemed to search for words "—tall."

"You can tell by where my voice is coming from?"

"Yes. Almost a head taller than I am."

His lips were only inches from her hair, and they itched to press against her. He wanted to breathe her in without any space between them, but he resisted.

"What else can you tell about me?" he asked, knowing that taking away one of her senses, like her sight, would sharpen the others.

"You smell like leather. Like you spend time outside...or maybe inside. The leather could be from the fancy furniture. And your hands...they're strong. Big. Like maybe you work with them."

That was true in his off-hours at his main home, a gentleman's ranch up in Cambria, where he tended the horses. Otherwise, he was either at his desk with its computer or traveling, going from one investment to another: a new golf resort near Dallas, a start-up solar company in Nevada, a software company here in SoCal....

Not that she needed to know any of this.

He wanted her to feel more of his hands, so he slowly slid one from her shoulder to her neck. She gasped as he rested his palm at the base of her throat, strumming his fingers over her pulse.

It throbbed, echoing inside his own body, everywhere.

"What would you think," he said, "if you felt my hands all over you?"

She laughed, again nervously. "More foreplay?"

"A lot more."

He thought he heard a sound of surrender as he brushed her throat with his fingertips. His groin was pumping with a desire he could barely contain, his lungs so tight that he could barely talk anymore.

So he didn't talk. Instead, he brought his other hand to the side of her head, angling it so her neck was exposed to his mouth. But he didn't kiss her.

Too early. Too intimate.

He only allowed his breath to coat her skin as he listened to her own breathing quicken. Then he eased the hand at her throat down, over a breast, feeling how her nipple beaded beneath her thin blouse and her bra.

Rubbing his thumb around it, he held her as her knees gave out.

"That's my beautiful girl," he whispered in her ear, disturbing some strands of blond hair that had escaped from her braid. "Just give in."

"I already have." She reached up, bringing the hand he'd used to tilt her head down to her belly. "I know what I want from you, Callum. And I want it bad."

Was she saying what he thought she was saying?

At the idea of actually entering her, flesh to flesh, he froze. A sense of betrayal clutched at him, because he'd told himself that he wouldn't go that far with any woman, not even Leigh.

So he merely drew circles over her lower stomach with his fingers, toying with her breast with the other hand, making her press back against him. She'd be able to feel his erection through his jeans.

Damn it, he was ready, aching, but ever since Carla had died, there hadn't been anyone....

Not the time to think about that.

He brought his hand up so he could unbutton Leigh's blouse from the top down. One button. Another. He mimicked the teasing pace she'd used the other night when she'd undone the top of that country dress for him.

When he'd finished with the buttons, he drew the blouse from her shoulders, smoothing the material down her arms, letting it drop to the floor. Meanwhile, she hadn't made a move to take off her blindfold, but he knew it was because she'd bought fully into the game they were playing.

The perfect partner for what both of them needed— nothing but a good time.

With her blouse off, the sun coming through the window showed him the details of her back, streamlined and graceful, with muscles that defined her body, a slim waist. Unhooking her pink bra, he let that fall away from the front of her.

He gently turned her around so she faced him. He saw her mouth first—the pretty pink lips that parted with every short breath, the strong chin with the near dimple, the slant of her cheekbones under smooth skin. He wished he could remove the blindfold so he could look into her eyes, see what color they were up close, even though Beth had told him they were an olive-green.

Instead, he gazed down at her breasts. Small yet firm, tipped by coral areolae that had gone hard for him.

Cupping her with his palms, he ran both thumbs over her nipples, watching them peak.

"How many men have done this to you?" he asked.

"I don't want to think of other men."

"I want to know." He needed the mental distance that her past stories would provide.

"A few men. Not many. Not like this...."

She gasped again as he bent down and took a nipple into his mouth. Losing her balance, she planted her hands in his hair, grasping it while he used his tongue to swirl around her.

"Callum..." she murmured.

The sound of another man's name pierced him, and he took his mouth off of her.

Why had it mattered? Why should it, when this was what they'd both signed up for?

He stood, her fingers still entwined in his hair, feeling its texture as if that would give her a clue as to what he looked like.

He let her do it until his chest got warm, and then he grabbed her by the wrists, lowering her hands. But he dived right back into the game as he trailed his fingers down her ribs, her waist, coming to where her wraparound skirt tied. With an aggressive tug, he undid that, and the material twisted to the ground, leaving her in just her blindfold, pink lace panties and boots. He could see a hint of hair beneath the pink, and the sight needled his cock.

Hooking his thumbs in the sides of her underwear, he raised the material up so it pressed against the center of her, and she fisted her hands by her sides. Then he pulled the material down, over her thighs, her knees, her boots. She stepped out of the panties, holding her hands out so she wouldn't fall.

Damn, she was pretty everywhere—pink in her center, fine blond hair covering her. He helped her off with her boots and, controlling himself, setting the pace, he went to the bed.

"Where are you?" she asked.

When he looked back at her, she had her hands in front of her, searching for him.

"Right here." He moved back to her with the negligee in hand. "Raise your arms."

As soon as she did, he lowered the garment over her, and he could see her shiver as the filmy material whisked along her skin.

"Come here," he said, taking her hand and leading her to the bed, sitting her down. Then he bent to a knee, taking one stocking, sliding it up her leg. It was the kind that had sticky stuff that held up the silk, so he didn't have to fasten any garters.

He skimmed the second one up her other leg, trying hard not to look at the pink between her thighs again. But it was nearly impossible.

Grabbing her hand once more, he helped her up from the bed, turned her around, then decided to forget about the matching robe. He wanted as much skin as possible to go with the negligee.

"You comfortable?" he asked.

"Yes. I kind of wish I could see what I look like, though. I've never worn lingerie that feels this nice."

For a second he wondered if she was still getting used to her new appearance, all the weight she'd lost. But she would've looked just as good with those extra curves as she did now.

"You'd be pleased with what you see, just like I am," he said. "Remember when I mentioned the satin doll?"

She nodded.

"That's you," he said. "A living doll to admire."

"A blow-up doll who won't kiss and tell?"

"No." In spite of their no-strings-attached arrangement, she wasn't just an object to him. Then again, that was how this whole thing had started out, wasn't it? With her being a challenge, a Taste of Honey date that wouldn't last for more than a night. But somewhere along the line, that idea had gone off the rails, and he was trying to get it back on.

And he would, just as he controlled everything else in his life: the finances he'd tripled since inheriting them from Carla, his emotions when it came to meeting women online or going on a so-called blind date like this....

He led Leigh toward the window, where a silk damask upholstered chair with thick mahogany armrests and legs waited. Sitting her down, he backed away.

"I'm going to dress you a little more," he said.

"In what?"

"I'll tell you as I'm doing it."

As she reclined in the chair, he snatched the toe shoes from the mattress. Beth, who'd taken ballet lessons in her youth, had shown him how to tie them after he'd ordered all the different outfits and had them express delivered.

He carefully eased the slippers onto Leigh's feet, wrapping the long satin strands around one ankle, then the next.

"And something else." He fetched the last detail from the bed.

"Just tell me," she said.

"Trust me, remember?" He took a silken cord and laid it over her wrist. "Do you know what this is?"

"I remember seeing it on the mattress." A mere whisper.

"I won't do this if you don't want it."

She hesitated, and he almost backed off, disappointment heavy in his belly.

Then she leaned her head back on the chair.

"Try it," she said, and he heard how the excitement laced her voice now.

A first time for everything, he thought. And he would make her first time worthwhile.

He secured her wrists with both cords, then guided one of her feet to the leg of the chair.

"Is this okay?" he asked.

She must've felt the air brushing against the center of her thighs, because she'd let her head cant to the side in obvious restlessness.

"Yes," she said.

Keeping himself in line, he avoided looking at anything but her ankle as he tied her, then worked on the other one.

When he was done, her legs were parted, her toes en pointe just like a ballerina's, her most private place clearly damp with excitement.

But there was more. So much more.

He lifted a feather from the bed, waiting. One minute. One minute and a half.

"Where are you?" she asked anxiously.

"Here."

"What're you doing?"

"Wondering where you think I'm going to touch you now."

"Callum, this isn't fair. You're killing me."

He was feeling a little death creeping up on him more and more, too. "Don't worry about anything."

He touched the feather to her cheek, and she jumped.

"Something soft," he said. "Something harmless."

"The feather I saw near the cords."

"That's right."

Trailing it downward, he coasted it over her collarbone, between her breasts, and then he pulled it away.

She was trembling, sinking down in her seat, her back arched as she strained against the cords.

"Are there any men in your life now, Leigh?" he asked.

She blew out a breath. "Are you asking about my love life again?"

"Just idle talk." And distance.

"Of course there aren't."

"Because you're a free agent."

"That's right."

"Why, though?" He could see her hips wiggling a bit, as if inviting him to put the feather on her again. "Any man would be lucky to have you."

She gritted her jaw, and he knew she was probably thinking, *Then why're you waiting?*

He laughed, taking mercy on her, using the feather again, guiding it under a breast. She pressed toward it, whimpering slightly. And when he brushed it back and forth over her nipple, she parted her lips, churning her hips slightly.

That drew his attention to her spread legs, her glistening center just under the see-through creamy white material. She was open to him, her clit stiff and ready.

His erection beating with need, he lightly touched the feather to her pleasure spot.

"Damn you," she murmured, pulling against her bindings.

"Should I stop?"

"Yes. No. Don't stop."

He wanted to ask her to reach back into her memories, to tell him if she remembered that one party where a boy with dark hair, gold eyes and broadening shoulders under a plaid shirt had longed for her. But the memory of those days, when he'd been a nobody, before Carla had come along and made him feel like a somebody, caused such weakness. And weakness wasn't a part of his life anymore.

He bent down, untying the cords at her ankles with jerky motions, then effortlessly hooked her legs over his shoulders. A little cry came from her as he pulled her hips to his mouth, making her rock toward him as he connected with her.

Wet. Strawberry. Leigh.

Kissing her between the legs thoroughly, he slowly worked her, using his lips, his tongue. She squirmed under him, moaning, grinding against him.

He even thought he heard some cursing as he entered her with his tongue, in and out, sucking, then circling her clit.

As her voice got higher, his libido did, too, slicing upward with a vicious stroke of passion, darting sideways and back again, slashing desire through him until he had to hold back from bursting.

Another violent cut upward…another rip through his belly…up, up, up—

Just as he thought he couldn't take any more, she let out a full-throated cry that seemed to echo through every corner of the room. His cock pushed against his jeans, and he knew that he needed satisfaction now or a release outside of this room, away from her.

"I want you inside me," she said, her voice rough. "Now, Callum…."

He wanted it, too. Damn it, did he ever. But that hadn't been in his plans. It couldn't be.

He'd never forgive himself if he went that far, although with every beat of his pulse, he needed her and wanted to make her feel like the most desirable woman on earth.

Before he did something he would be sorry for, he grabbed the robe from the bed, laying it over her legs, then untied her wrists just before he left the room for the release his body was keening for. But as usual, he hadn't had enough from Leigh.

Would he ever?

LEIGH WAS JUST coming down from her crackling high when she realized that her hands were untied and she was alone.

No sound in the room. No Callum. Or was she wrong? "Callum?"

Nothing. She fumbled with her blindfold, pulling it down, her body still on fire.

"Callum?"

Still no answer. Really? Even after all that, he wasn't going to stick around? She'd been almost sure that he was leading up to a huge "Hey, I'm the guy who just gave you the Big O" moment and would reveal himself this time.

But it was all part of the game. He'd given her a screaming orgasm yet hadn't gotten off himself. Maybe he was saving that for tonight…?

She stood, losing her balance once again, but this time because of the ballet shoes. Nonetheless, she tossed the blindfold to the bed. Then, across the room, she noticed a full-length old-fashioned mirror, and she stopped moving when she got a gander at herself.

Was this actually her? The slim woman with the long blond braid, dressed in a naughty angel's negligee and thigh-high stockings?

A flush roared up her body, bathing her face red, when she took in just how skimpy her outfit was. But...

She looked the way almost every female wanted to look—like a model out of a lingerie catalog. Everything society told her was attractive in a woman.

One of the cords was hanging from her wrist, and she glanced at it, then shook it off just as she was shaking off the thought about the lingerie models.

The house was too quiet, and belatedly, she recalled the raging cry she'd given out when she'd climaxed. Was *now* the time for some embarrassment?

No. She still couldn't sink into it all the way. Why should she anyway, when this was what her body had been made for? She'd only started realizing it now, with Callum. And, God help her, she wondered what would happen tonight with him if this was just a warm-up.

Exhaling, she peeled off the slippers, stockings, then the negligee, giving all of them a wistful glance before leaving them on the bed. She got back into her regular clothes with almost a sense of regret.

To think—she regretted dressing instead of undressing with this guy. Her world was totally upside down.

After grabbing the phone he'd given her and looking both ways before entering the hallway, she decided that no one had been around to hear her give that banshee-sex yell earlier, and she went back to her room, shutting the door behind her.

She itched to call Margot or Dani but decided against it. Maybe for once in her life, she could enjoy her secrets, keeping them to herself since she'd never really had any before. But as she went to her window and looked at the afternoon sun, she wondered what she could do now to top the experience she'd just had. It was still hours before dinner.

Should she relax and watch the flat-screen TV in the room? Pick up the house phone and have someone prep the spa room for her, even if she wasn't sure what was in that spa room? Wander around the house and snoop? Yeah, that'd be polite. Besides, she suspected that this house had no trace of Callum, so there wasn't much use in going Sherlock on him.

How about the pool, though? Couldn't she use a good turn in the hot tub?

Let Callum watch her strut out there in a bathing suit. That would get him pumped up for more....

Digging into her suitcase, she came out with a demurely flowered two-piece bikini and a purple cover-up with flip-flops. After fixing her hair into a loose bun, she grabbed a towel from the bathroom and stepped into the dim hallway again.

She guessed where the pool was based on its location relative to the "nookie room," as she'd come to think of it—the room with a view and a whole lot of stories to tell after today. But just as she came to the wrought-iron pool gate, she paused, suddenly hit with a question.

The blindfold...Callum not wanting her to see him. Was it possible that he was scarred somehow and that was why he wasn't showing himself?

She almost laughed that off. Melodramatic much?

But then a far more realistic question came on its heels: Was she the first woman Callum had played these games with?

Now, that made her feel…well, ridden hard and put away wet. He'd made her feel special on their dates, and to think that this might be his typical M.O. with all women was disheartening, to say the least.

When she got to the hot tub, she easily found the control panel, letting the water bubble to life, dipping her toe into it.

Her skin sang, reawakened by the heat, making her remember all too piercingly what Callum had just done to her.

Or not done.

No matter, she thought, taking off her cover-up and flip-flops. She'd just gotten to the ranch. He had to be saving the best for last.

As she recalled his hands on her, a wave of brave hedonism took her over, and she looked around. Nobody was here. But was Callum watching?

She thought of the bindings, the dress-up clothes, the feather and the blindfolds. He was into some real kink, that much was obvious. And she wanted some of that, too.

But she was outside, in front of God and country. Did she have the guts for some of her own kink?

Why not?

She stripped off her bathing suit top, tossing it carelessly aside. Then, with a purposeful look at the house, her gaze locking on what she thought was the nookie-room window, she stepped out of her bottoms.

Take that, Callum, she thought, reveling in the feel

of sun over her bare skin. She even got a little extra naughty and stretched her arms over her head. It was a beautiful, warm day, and she was feeling sexy. She was feeling watched...and liking it.

Then she entered the sunken tub. The water swirled around her feet, her calves, her thighs.... When it lapped at the middle of her legs, she bit her lip, staying there for a moment, imagining Callum.

His mouth, on her, nibbling, sucking....

With a tiny groan, she eased all the way in, breathing a satisfied sigh.

Only in southern California could she be in a hot tub in November, she thought. Only with Callum could she be so wicked.

A sense of loss pricked her at the notion of this being so temporary. She wished...

What? That she could always be with him?

That wasn't their deal.

Just relax. Enjoy. Have the biggest adventure you'll ever have right here and right now.

Leigh sat back and luxuriated in the water, listening to the tumble and flow of it.

She didn't even know Callum was there until she felt what was becoming a familiar sensation by now—a blindfold sliding over her eyes.

"Shhh," he said.

"Callum?" Duh.

He rested his hand on the sensitive area between her throat and shoulder, and she melted.

"It occurred to me," he said in that voice, "that you might need some finishing to what we started. So I came down here to do just that."

8

WITH THE WATER fluttering at her skin and the blindfold over her eyes again, Leigh was caught in his net, drowning in his sensual suggestions, lost in the erotic darkness he brought her every time he blindfolded her.... However you said it, she was a goner.

"Were you keeping an eye on me from the house?" she asked.

"Would it make you even wetter if I said yes?"

She was already there, her clit stiff and beating.

"And what would you tell me," he said, his mouth close to her ear, "if I wanted to film you this time?"

Leigh didn't know what to say for a moment. She was filmed all the time for her show, but this wasn't remotely the same. He wanted her naked on film, recorded for the ages. Her common sense told her no, but she was far, far beyond that.

She said, "Why would you want to do that?"

"Why would any man?" He laughed, disturbing the stray wisps of hair by her ears with his soft breath. "Looking at you makes me crazy, Leigh, and to look at you again and again while you're coming? That makes me even crazier."

This was crazy. Then again, it wasn't. Maybe this was how she should've been all along—insanely deviant, deliriously craving him.

"Yes," she said, just as she always said to him. She wasn't even sure where she would draw the line anymore, because she loved the thought of making him happy. It made her happy, too. If there was ever a time when it didn't…then she would draw that line, but not before.

His hand tightened on her, and she wished she could see his face. But all she could do was imagine dark hair and hungry brown eyes.

Then he left her for a moment. He was setting up the recording device—a smartphone? A tablet? A digital camera? Whatever it was, she was about to be the star.

Number one in his world for this short time.

Even as that thought made her heart sink again—why, when leaving him was inevitable?—her ears picked up another sound.

Something being poured into the water?

When she smelled flowers—bubble bath?—and then felt a foamy cloud brush by her, she knew she was right.

"I said I wanted to pamper you," he whispered, his lips next to her ear again. "How about a little of this?"

She felt something soft and cushiony on her shoulder, and she pictured everything: his big hands holding a pink sponge; his nails, blunt and smooth as he gripped it; his skin, tanned. He still smelled like leather, and it made her senses tilt.

He took his time with her, bathing her neck as she leaned her head back. Wiping over her upper chest as she relaxed to the sound of water trickling from the sponge. Rivulets streamed down her skin, tickling her.

"Found a dirty spot," he said, going lower, slipping the sponge below the curve of her naked breast.

She reared up at the contact, her nipple pebbling painfully. "I think all of me is a dirty spot around you."

He laughed again—she loved that she made him do that—and he washed her thoroughly, taking care with both her breasts especially, then rubbing her stomach and slipping down farther.

When he got to her achiest part, she was terribly ready. Her legs parted as he slid an arm down and around her waist, lifting her up so that she was kneeling on the cement bench underneath the water.

Bubbles frothed against her thighs, adding an extra layer of pleasure while he massaged her between the legs with the sponge.

"You were frustrated when I left you earlier," he said against her ear. His words were like a vibration that ate its way to her belly, threatening to make her come again. "You wanted more."

"Did you mean to leave me that way?" she asked.

He didn't say anything, just pressed the sponge up and against her clit, making her whimper. When he circled there, her hips shifted with every movement.

Finally, he answered. Sort of.

"I'm going to give you more, Leigh. You'll just have to wait a little longer."

One of his hands was cupping her breast as he continued to work her between the legs, and she leaned her face against his arm. The material of his shirt was wet, and she would've given anything to have seen how the cotton plastered against his skin. She also would've died to bring him into the tub with her, but those weren't the rules of this game.

And if anything, she was getting to be such a good player.

Heat was rising in her like a push of restless water, and she was getting close...so close....

When he took the sponge away, she protested.

"Shhh," he said again. "Just wait. It's all about the waiting."

Was that how he rolled? Making his women wait until he was ready?

Just as she was about to say something to him about it, she heard a humming sound.

And when he slid a long, smooth object down her arm, she knew what it was...and that it had to be waterproof.

First he took the vibrator and swept it ever so gently over her nipple. Just enough so that it was like a whisper, a mere shiver.

"Callum," she said, asking for more in other places, places that were weeping and hurting and...

He pressed his lips against her ear, then sucked her lobe inside his mouth, warm, wet, swirling his tongue while submerging the vibrator under the water and over her belly.

And did he know the right place to use it—just above her mons. She quaked inside, not knowing how much longer she could last.

The combination of him sucking on one of her biggest erogenous zones and the vibrator down in taboo territory was making pinwheels of color revolve on her eyelids, and she slipped down into the water. The only thing holding her up was his arm.

"Not yet," he said, still pressed to her ear. "A little longer...."

She made a sound of desperation, but he was cruel, taking the vibrator and resting it at the very center of her, between her folds, over her clit.

The vibrator had nubs, causing sweet friction, and she heaved in a breath and grasped for the edge of the tub.

Too much. And too little. She wanted *him* inside her. Wanted it so badly.

Tiny bangs in her belly were counting up to an orgasm, but somehow he was stretching her out, definitely making her wait. Yet she was close to begging him for it. She wouldn't do it, though—that was probably why he was playing this game with her, wanting to see if she begged.

Instead, she pressed her face against his arm even harder, biting—not enough to break skin, but enough.

Of course, he laughed, but he sounded surprised, too. Just as turned on as she was.

"I think that means you're ready," he said.

She wondered if she would always be, just for him.

When he eased the vibrator up and into her, the buzzing sensation made her cry out. Instead of biting him, she was digging her nails into his muscled arm, grinding her hips as he moved the length in and out of her.

"Damn you," she said against him. *"Damn you."*

If he said anything in return, she didn't hear it. Her hearing had been blocked by the thud of her pulse, which mocked the one deep in her core.

Boom...boom...

In and out, humming, making her shiver inside with prickles that were building into an enormous shudder.

Boom, boom...

Her body felt as if it were starting to fall to pieces, dusting apart like sparkling debris.

Boom, boom—

As she banged all the way apart, she felt as liquid as the water, becoming one with it while she fell down, down into its embrace.

When Callum brought her out of the water with a giant sucking splash, she gasped for air, clinging to him.

Just as much in the dark as she'd ever been with that blindfold still over her eyes.

LIKE LAST TIME, he disappeared as stealthily as he'd appeared. But unlike last time, he'd caressed her and held her as she recovered.

Still blinded by the material over her eyes as well as her need for him. Still addicted.

There hadn't been much to say afterward, only some awkward laughter while she joked about the force of her orgasm. Then she'd made as much small talk as she could.

"What's next?" she'd asked. "That's up to you," he'd said. And she'd mentioned something about going to the stables to pass the time until dinner, which she would let someone else make for him tonight. Maybe she'd do breakfast for him?

All the while, she'd been hoping he'd tell her what *he* wanted next. Naturally, he hadn't. He kept her in the dark in more ways than one.

Before he'd left, he'd done something curious—touching her face with his fingertips, as if memorizing this moment.

But why would he do that when he had it all on film?

After he'd gone and she'd taken off the blindfold—not before the five minutes he'd asked her to wait had passed—she'd dried off with a towel from the pool house. Then she'd gone to her room, where she'd dazedly put on some jeans, a long shirt and her boots.

Was she only one of many girls who'd gone through this with him before? She couldn't stop thinking of that, couldn't stop wondering why it was starting to matter more and more as this date went on.

But that was the wrong approach to take, wasn't it? Callum had given her something she'd never expected when she'd auctioned off that basket: some confidence. She still wasn't sure she could always keep off her weight, but why did it matter with Callum? He'd never see her in person if she gained those pounds back and she would never witness his reaction. In the end, she decided, he'd at least given her some light inside of herself. She could shine it on the person she wanted to be right here, right now.

She could do anything with him and never regret it.

After going downstairs, she headed in the direction that Callum had instructed her to go earlier before they'd said ta-ta. When she saw the stables, she felt like her old self again and not the pampered guest that Callum had made her: she was the girl who loved horses and who went for long rides when she was at home.

It didn't take her long to find a beaut of a mare in the stalls—a paint with big dark eyes—and she fell in love right away.

"Hey, darlin'," she said, reaching out her hand and allowing the animal to sniff it, getting to know her.

Footsteps sounded behind her, and she backed away from the stall to avoid spooking the horse. Callum had sneaked up on her earlier. What if he was doing the same thing now?

She turned around. A man was standing near an office door, leaning against the frame with his Stetson tilted back on his dark head and his gold eyes gleaming. His skin was a rosy-tan hue, as if he had some south-of-the-border in him, and...

Leigh's pulse jittered just looking at him. A tall-drink-of-water cowboy, right here in front of her.

Callum?

But then he spoke, his Western accent thick, his voice not Callum's at all. "That's Bessie Blue. I think she's taken a shine to you."

The man stuck out his hand, coming toward her to introduce himself.

"My name's Adam," he said.

HE WAS GOING to hell for this, wasn't he?

But after Leigh had let him know that she intended to visit the stables, the idea had slammed into Adam, and he'd run with it.

Would it really do any harm to take their date a twisty step further? What if he could meet her one time only, face-to-face, as a regular guy? It'd be the *only* time, and then he'd go back to being Callum.

The idea sounded stranger than anything he'd done with Leigh so far, but, heaven help him, as soon as the notion had hit him, he'd realized how much he wanted to see the color of her eyes without a blindfold. Yet a more perverse side had wanted to know how she would react to seeing *him,* the guy from college. And as soon as he'd thought of it, he'd known that this would give him some peace of mind, tying up the loose ends of his fascination for her and allowing him to let go of it once she went home.

No harm in it, he'd thought.

So he'd told Jerry, the regular groom, that he could spend the rest of the day off. Adam had easily taken over his position on the ranch since he was more than familiar with how one ran. But first he'd changed his shirt, which had gotten wet during his latest rendezvous with Leigh.

The hot tub…the bubbles…the nail marks she'd left on his arm, causing him pleasurable pain….

But he could just hear his best friend and conscience now if she knew what he was up to.

"Unbelievable," Beth would say. "Now I know for certain that you've got a heart of stone."

But he could withstand the lash of words. He would merely tell his confidante that there was nothing romantic going on with Leigh.

God, even in his head his excuses sounded flat. Maybe he *did* have a heart of stone these days. Granite, more likely.

He didn't need Beth to tell him that, or that he was probably pulling this stunt because he wanted Leigh to know that this was him without really telling her. In a way, he was even reliving that party from his freshman year, and he wanted to see if she would get a sparkle in her eye if she recognized him.

In some bent way, games like this allowed him to keep a canyon between him and any woman he was attracted to.

See? He didn't need a shrink to tell him what was what. He already knew damned well.

But what the hell had possessed him to make this date even more dangerous than it already was? It was probably because he wanted to see if his real name rang any kind of bell in Leigh. And as she'd run her gaze over him, Adam had thought for a hot moment that she *had* recognized the college boy he'd been then.

Yet in the aftermath of that first gaze, he hadn't seen any sign of recognition on her face at all, and with a combination of disappointment and relief, he'd made his way to her, holding out his hand in greeting.

When she introduced herself, her cheeks were flushed, just as they had been in the bedroom after he'd put the blindfold on her the first time. And her eyes…

They were the most astonishing shade of dark green he'd ever seen.

Altogether, she was a breath of fresh air with her smile and that playful little dimple in her chin, and it was nearly surreal standing in front of her like this— two people under normal circumstances meeting each other. A cowgirl and a cowboy—one who dressed this way only when he retreated to this ranch.

Suddenly, taking this chance as Adam was worth every bit of risk.

They shook hands, and as his skin met hers, fire burned between them—and it had nothing to do with sexual innuendo or kinky expectation. This was Leigh and Adam finally meeting, just as he wished they had all those years ago.

But if that had happened, he might not have met Carla.

Just thinking about that made his heart dive, and he let go of Leigh's hand. A laden instant hung between them, and he noticed that her flush was still going strong.

Was she…interested in Adam?

A gnarled flash of jealousy struck him even though

Adam was Callum and Callum was Adam. Still, something green and spiky revolved in his belly.

He gestured toward Bessie Blue, who'd been hanging her head over her stall gate, checking out Leigh. "We bought her at an auction a few months ago. She's got a gentle disposition with some fire." He knew all this because he'd been the one who'd purchased Bessie.

"Sounds like a girl I could get along with." Leigh couldn't keep her hands off the horse, and the animal adored her right back.

Something in Adam's chest seemed to expand at the connection between the two. It'd been forged quickly and easily. But why not, when both were bighearted?

She didn't seem all that much in a hurry to wander around, lingering instead with Bessie. "Can I ask you something?"

"Shoot."

"Whose house is this?"

Adam held back a smile. This woman didn't give up. Or was she so perceptive that she'd taken one look at his dark hair and allowed her imagination to assume that he might be Callum?

Adrenaline gave him a jolt, so he dodged the question. "I've been warned not to answer your more direct queries, miss."

"Call me Leigh. And damn. It sounds like you've been recruited to the dark side. Callum has some real loyal people on his payroll."

He got a bit of a glow from that. Her opinion mattered. "Callum can be pretty persuasive. And," he added just for good measure, "a nice guy to boot." He hadn't been able to help himself.

"You must have some kind of Christmas bonus coming," she said, laughing.

This close to her, that laughter sounded crystal clear, and it cut straight through to his gut, just as it had the night at the college party. He held on to his resolve, though, planting his hands on his hips, smiling. From the corner of his eye, he realized that the sun was starting to scoop down in the sky. Leigh would be off to the house for dinner all too soon, and she'd probably expect Callum to be there, chatting with her on the phone.

"So how long have you worked here?" she asked.

"About as long as Bessie Blue's been in that stall." Even Adam needed a fictional story. "In short, not very."

Bessie Blue looked as though she was in paradise as Leigh kept petting her. "Then you really don't know much about Callum."

He chuckled. "If I didn't know any better, I'd say you're doing something undercover here. Are you a reporter?" Or was she trying to catch him in a lie and finger him as Callum?

"I'm just a guest." She seemed surprised that he didn't know the reasons for her stay.

Her phone dinged, probably with a text message, and he almost shouted a hallelujah. But he'd gotten himself in this position, and he should've expected that she'd put a lot of heat on him.

She checked out her screen. "A message from one of my producers. I can get to this later."

"Don't mind me. You go on ahead."

"Nah. I'm on vacation. It's unfortunate that it's probably too late to go on a ride here with Bessie Blue, huh?"

The horse nickered.

"'Fraid so. If you want to saddle up tomorrow, I can

arrange that, but it'll get dark fast, and you don't want to be caught out there alone on trails you aren't familiar with."

For a second he thought that she might ask him to join her on a ride, and he wasn't sure that was a good idea.

So he scrambled.

"How about I walk you down to the house?" he said instead. He needed to get back into Callum's shoes anyway. "And we'll talk about what time is good for you to hit the trails tomorrow."

"Sounds good, Adam."

As she shared a fond goodbye with Bessie Blue, Adam took a moment to wallow in how good it felt for her to say his real name.

As LEIGH WALKED by Adam's side to the house, she left a space between them.

Most of her suspicions about him being Callum had abated when he'd started talking in that drawl. He didn't even move as Callum probably did—like a panther in the night. And Adam didn't seem to have half Callum's confidence. Besides, Callum had brown eyes, not gold like Adam's.

But she'd asked him questions anyway, and he'd answered convincingly enough. It was the drawl that made her think he was just a guy who worked on the ranch, though. It was far from Callum's tenor.

At any rate, Adam was rugged, handsome…a dish that she had no business eyeing. And she'd been trying not to do it ever since she'd met him in the stables.

What had Callum done to her hormones anyway? Shifted them into high gear? God help her if he'd given her so much sexual va-va-voom that she couldn't compose herself around any handsome guy she happened to come in contact with over the next few days.

Callum was her host, and she wasn't about to two-time him, even mentally. Even if there was nothing serious between them. Lusting after some other guy just wasn't...decent.

When they came to the deck that overlooked the pool area, Adam, who'd kept his chatter to the subject of riding during the entire walk, paused.

"This is where I leave you," he said.

She grinned at him in thanks, but he glanced away before she blushed too hard, damn her.

Get it under control, she thought. *Callum's your date, and frankly, you can barely even handle* him.

What would someone like Adam think if the Mystery Man decided to call her on the disposable phone right now? Was he even privy to how Callum operated? She almost wished Callum would call, just to see the look on Adam's face—and to know for sure if the groom was in on current events.

He'd taken off his cowboy hat, holding it low in both hands. She noticed that his hair was boyishly ruffled, but she ignored that little detail.

"Well," Adam said, "you have a good night."

"No doubt I will. You, too."

Silence. He didn't seem in a hurry to get anywhere.

Just as she was about to leave, he spoke up.

"I hear you're a celebrity."

Ah. So the staff did know a bit about her. "Not really. If they had a Z-list, that's what I'd be on."

Adam was frowning, as if he wanted to say something. It reminded Leigh of how Callum had told her earlier that she should be proud of her accomplishments.

He was right.

"I guess I make the home crowd proud." She smiled. "And a few others."

"You guess?"

Leigh tried not to let his drawl seep into her. She'd always had crushes on the more down-to-earth type growing up. Being attracted to a rich man like Callum, whose tone was so smooth and polished, proved the exception.

"Actually, my parents have never been grand with their praise," Leigh said, and although her tone was light, she felt a faint heaviness. "But that's okay. To tell the truth, I dedicate my show to my sister. If you ever watch and then look hard enough, you'll always see her name in the credits."

"Your sister..."

"Died years and years ago."

Adam's golden gaze was soft as he looked at her, then looked away again.

"That must've been an awful time for you," he said.

There was something about him that made it okay to say, "It was. She'd just gotten home from college for summer vacation, and she was getting together with old friends at the swimming hole on our property. She was a good swimmer, so her drowning was a shock. But someone brought beer, and her friends said she'd never had a drink before. She went into the water for some reason, and no one even noticed as they carried on with the party. When someone did see her, it was too late."

There'd been so many dark days after that, her parents almost forgetting that Leigh was still alive. Everything she'd done—graduating as the valedictorian, acing her college classes, winning community-service awards with the sorority—had paled next to perfect Hannah and what she *could've* accomplished.

Always second place. The only time Leigh had felt as if she'd pulled out of it was with Callum, who was giving her a new lease on life.

Adam glanced toward the stables, as if she'd gotten too personal and he wanted to get back. His tone was flat as he said, "It seems there's no getting through life without losing someone precious at some point."

Leigh waited for him to offer more, but he never did. Instead, he put his hat back on and nodded to her, walking away.

It wasn't until she was inside the house that she realized that his tone had been just as dark as his boss's was, but she brushed away the thought when the phone Callum had given her rang.

9

After Adam had gone a safe distance away, near the guesthouse he'd holed up in, he'd called Leigh to let her know that his housekeeper, Mrs. Ellison, was cooking dinner and Leigh was welcome to have cocktails at the fully stocked bar in the study while she waited.

Then he'd ventured back to the stables to close up shop for the night while Leigh ate. But there was an even better excuse to retreat there.

For the second time that day, he'd given out too much information: first he'd used his own name with Leigh; then he'd commented about losing someone precious.

It was just that he'd felt for her. He understood that kind of pain, especially when the person left you when she was still so young and vital.

Two years and counting since Carla had gone, he thought, sitting in the stable office with the lights on dim, the horses content in their stalls. Except for Bessie Blue, who kept looking at the entrance as if hoping Leigh would come back.

"I know how you feel," he murmured, thinking of Leigh, thinking of how his body missed her and how he couldn't go another hour without her. Sure, the feeling would pass, but while she was here, he couldn't stay away.

And, as it ended up, he didn't.

When he checked in with Mrs. Ellison a couple of hours later, she told him that she was off to her nearby home. Leigh had enjoyed the pan-fried steak with marsala sauce and all the trimmings, but she was pretty sure his guest had been lonely eating by herself.

Duly chided, he thanked her for her work, then hung up. He'd decided not to call Leigh during dinner. That was all a part of the game, wasn't it? Make her wait, make her anticipate until she couldn't stand it anymore. It'd worked with her earlier, bringing her to a climax in the hot tub so provocatively that he had the nail marks on his arm to prove it.

So why wouldn't it work now?

After he'd cleaned up, he stood in the guesthouse cottage, with its cream-and-beige upholstery and dark wood. He looked out the window toward the big house, where Leigh would be, yes, waiting.

He dialed his disposable phone and, as if making *him* suffer a bit, too, she picked up after several rings.

"Who is it?"

"You don't know by now?"

"Oh. I thought Callum had disappeared off the face of the earth."

He laughed, mostly because he deserved her feistiness. "The meal was to your satisfaction?"

"Yes. Your Mrs. Ellison can cook. But I have to say that there was one thing to complain about."

He waited again, damn her.

"Dessert," she finally said. "I didn't get enough of it. And here I am in my room wishing I could have more."

Funny, he thought. Leigh was getting pretty good at playing him as well as he played her.

"What're you in the mood for?" he asked, his voice gravelly.

Now it was her turn to pause. And by the time she answered, his heartbeat was double-timing.

"I was thinking," she said softly, enticingly, "that you might have something new for me to taste."

And that was all it took. He asked her if she had a blindfold handy, and when she said yes, he told her to put it on, then hung up, shoving the phone into his pants pocket, snatching the tablet where he'd transferred the film of Leigh he'd taken earlier. As a precaution, nothing else was stored on it, only their liaison.

He went to the house, taking care to stick to the shadows so she wouldn't see him if she was looking out her window. He sneaked in through a side door, turning off any lights that were on as he went. Taking the stairs, at one with the darkness, he came to her door, slowly easing it open a crack.

"Is it on?" he asked.

She didn't have to ask what he meant, and that was when he knew that she was just as tied up in their fantasies as he was, that they did something for her that she'd never felt before, and she didn't want to ruin the illusion.

"It's on," she said, and he took her meaning more than one way.

The blindfold was over her eyes.

And the night was definitely on.

Not that he didn't trust her, but he peered into the room before he stepped all the way inside. There she was, sitting on her bed blindfolded, her back to the door as she faced the window. The curtains were open only a sliver, allowing in a peek of night. It was dark, no moon, and all he could see were shadows and outlines. But her silhouette was what caught his eye.

Curvy yet slim, she was wearing a darkly sheer short negligee that she must've brought with her. The ties from the blindfold he'd used earlier trailed down her back, skimming the blond flow of her hair.

He closed the door behind him, and he could hear her exhale.

"I'm glad to see you didn't go against my wishes," he said. "You put the blindfold on as I asked."

"Maybe I like what you do to me, so I obey."

His cock was already thudding, agonizing him. He'd held back from entering her thus far for the sake of Carla's memory.

But now? It took all he had to restrain himself from striding over to Leigh and stripping off that negligee, then plunging into her heat, losing himself in her.

Steadying himself, he walked over to her. She sat so straight, hands on her lap, long legs pressed together. The blindfold covered her eyes.

He couldn't help it—there was something more going on now, a link of sorts that her candid admission about her sister had planted in him. She wasn't just a woman to have sex with.

But that was what she had to be if Adam was going to come out of this unscathed.

Before he touched her, he powered up the computer pad, then put it on an antique table, propping it against the wall.

"Tell me what's happening, Callum," she said. "I'm getting nervous."

"Isn't that half the fun?"

She laughed a little. "I suppose it is. My heart's going a hundred miles per hour, like it wants to pop out of me. It makes me want to do things that I…"

Taking a deep breath, she scooted forward ever so slightly to the edge of the mattress.

And when she reached toward him, he knew what she had in mind.

"You're always the one bringing me pleasure," she whispered. "Can I…?"

Without thinking, he stepped forward, close enough so that she must've felt him standing just inches from her hand.

Biting her lip, she blindly searched for him until she touched his thigh.

He stifled a groan. Even a soft touch like that made him die for her. And when she traced her hand back, over his hip, down his thigh, as if mapping him, he fisted his own hands.

"Muscles," she said. "I knew you'd have muscles everywhere."

She skimmed her fingers upward, to his waist, his belly, scooting forward another inch on the bed so she could reach his chest.

"Oh. Callum. Are you for real?"

Sometimes he wasn't sure. "What do you want to do next, Leigh? Tell me."

As she tilted her face up to him, he didn't have to see her eyes to know. Her hand said everything as she coasted it down his stomach, his belly, to his cock.

He almost blasted apart as she made contact. Blood

punched him, pushing his growing erection against his zipper.

"Now who's ready?" she asked teasingly. "And who'll be even readier when I'm through with him?"

He closed his eyes as if she'd put her own blindfold on *him*. It was almost the truth, too, because as she undid the button at the top of his fly, then unzipped him, his sight scrambled. All he was aware of was her fingers, gently taking him out of his pants, running down his length, killing him slowly.

She held him with one hand, using her other to coax a finger under his shaft. His fingernails dug into his palms.

"Everyone else has seen your face," she said, "but I get to know a whole different part of you. How well do you want me to get acquainted, Callum?"

He'd created a monster. "As well as you want."

She laughed softly as she circled her thumb over his tip. Moisture was dewing him there, and he didn't know how much more he could take.

And when she pressed her lips to his tip, he almost came right there, right then. The only thing saving him was the willpower he'd exercised all these years.

But she tested even that when she took him into her mouth, swirling her tongue around him, drawing back and sucking, then starting all over again.

That was when his mind went completely blank, and all he was aware of was cupping the back of her head, feeling her go back and forth, bathing him, building such a head of steam inside him that he gritted his jaw, fighting it some more. Fighting her.

Yet she didn't fight fair. She touched his sac with the tips of her fingers, and he was a goner, coming into her mouth, holding back curses and moans until he was spent.

As he floated back to reality, the room was filled with their ragged breathing, and he unwound his fingers from her hair, stroking her, feeling closer to her than he had with anyone in years.

Feeling the guilt of that.

He had to regain his footing with her, and he knew just how to do it.

Gathering all his strength—he wasn't going to let her know that the lining of his belly was shaking—he pulled away, grabbing a tissue and getting himself back together before zipping himself back inside his pants.

Then he accessed the tablet. "Your turn," he said.

As the film of them in the hot tub began playing, the sounds of seduction overtook everything else: his voice telling her that she made him crazy, the gurgle of water in the whirlpool, then the restless whimpers she made as he began to run the sponge over her.

He went to the other side of the bed, taking off his shirt on the way, letting it slump to the floor. When he got onto the mattress, it dipped with his weight, but she kept looking in the direction of that tablet, although she couldn't see it.

"Do you want to watch?" he asked as he came up behind her.

He saw her shiver, rubbing her hands over her arms. "Yes."

Gently, he reached in front of her, lifting up the blindfold slightly, just enough to give her an eyeful of the film. He'd focused the digital camera's lens on her, and all you could see of him were hands, arms covered with a water-steeped white shirt. He was cupping her breast from behind, making her nipple come to hardness.

Inspired, he did the same now, sliding his hand to her negligee-covered breast and palming it while his other hand held up the blindfold. He used his thumb to stimulate her, although she'd already been there when he'd started.

"You've played this over and over in your mind," he said. "Haven't you?"

"About a hundred times. And every time it ends the same way."

He knew what she meant—he always left before entering her. He told himself it would be the same tonight, but he wasn't so sure now.

Not while they watched her coming to a climax in the hot tub, crying out into his arm as she bit at him, clawed at him.

The film had taken up some time, but arousal had still come upon him quickly, with a hard-on so demanding that his sight was fragmenting again, making him think that he wasn't going to survive if he didn't feel her around him, embracing him, taking him into her velvet heat.

When she undid her negligee top, pulling it off so that he could feel her bared breast, his libido ticked as if it were a heater heading for an explosion.

Then she took his other hand—the one that had been lifting her blindfold—and brought it to her panties. Inside. Where she was slick for him.

She'd chosen not to see anymore, and even in his scattered mind, he knew the choice was bigger than it seemed.

She was still in the game.

As he slipped his fingers up and into her, making her arch, she twisted, pulling at her panties and somehow getting them off as she crawled all the way onto the mattress. Blood pumped him, driving him.

Tick, tick... Up and up went the pressure inside of him, urging him.

Just once, he thought. *Then it'll be over. We'll both be happy. We'll both move on....*

Tick, tick, tick...

At the sight of her fully naked body, the ticks turned into one long rattling inside of him, and he pulled her toward him, her chest to his, skin on skin as he kept churning his fingers into her, making her groan.

She clutched at him, bringing him down to the mattress with her as his body became one long prelude to a shudder. Then she groped under a pillow, coming out with a condom packet.

"I was hoping," she said.

He took his fingers out of her, snagging the condom, tearing into the packet and sheathing himself in record time. All the while, she blindly ran her hands over him, as if she couldn't get enough of feeling him.

And when he thrust into her, it was as if time suspended—him inside, her sucking in a breath at the sensation.

Tight, he thought. She was so tight that she surrounded him, and as he began to move inside her, she stayed with him, holding to him, her mouth parted in ecstasy.

Fascinated, he watched her face, even if he couldn't see her eyes. He didn't know he could still make someone feel like this. Hadn't really realized...

That there would be such feeling involved.

But something warm was taking him over, and it wasn't just sexual heat. It was in his chest, overcoming him, making him wish that he were normal like the Adam she'd met today in the stables.

Yet he wasn't, and he let go of that fantasy, giving in to this one as the promise of a cataclysmic shudder built, piling up on itself, up, up, up—

When he climaxed, it didn't take her long to do the same, and she still held on to him. He allowed himself to hold her, too, wondering, thinking…

No. He wasn't that other Adam. He was a guy who didn't do relationships, because they tore the soul out of you, never giving it back.

Leigh cuddled into his chest, her blindfold skimming his skin. "That time, the ending was a little different. It was a good ending, Callum."

But it could never be a happy ending with him, he thought as she eased into sleep.

And when he thought he couldn't stand the growing intimacy anymore, he drew away from her, looking at her face, which he could barely see in the near darkness. Just as he'd done earlier today, he touched it, feeling his chest constrict.

Then, pushing the emotion away, he left before he got to a point of no return.

ADAM RETREATED TO his guesthouse, sitting in a chair by the window, lonelier than he'd been in a long time, even if he'd just had mind-blowing sex with Leigh.

He had his phone out and had been staring at it for a while now, and he finally had the courage to bring up the one picture of his wife.

He'd banished the photos of her wearing scarves over

her balding head after chemo, still smiling, being brave for the camera. He hadn't recently looked at the albums packed away that she'd put together during their marriage, either—pictures of them at picnics, at the rodeo, laughing with each other, so in love that there'd never been a thought of death or destruction from the cancer that had eventually taken her.

But this one picture on his camera phone… He'd imported it to his cell's memory because he was so afraid it would someday fade from his own. An image of Carla on a carousel horse, her dress spread around her as she leaned into the pole, her dark hair flying while the ride spun in circles and made her laugh. He'd proposed to her that day.

The screen robbed him of the picture when it shut off, conserving power, but he still sat there, unable to get to sleep but so tired anyway.

Leigh would improve his mood if she were here. With her humor, she seemed to be the only person who knew how to shine a light deep down inside, where he was so dark and confused.

But he'd hotfooted it out of her bedroom, as usual.

He took a long shower, then came out dressed in pajama bottoms to sit on his bed. Staring at the phone. Resisting. Finally, inevitably giving in.

Leigh picked up on the third ring, and she sounded groggy. Why not, when she'd fallen asleep in his arms?

"Callum?"

"Sorry for waking you up."

"You didn't. Not really."

Was that some hurt he detected? Because he'd left her?

She added, "I slumbered off for a while with the… TV on. After I realized you'd gone, that is."

He sidestepped the last part. "The TV, huh?" He heard some sounds in the background—moans?—and then it switched off. He'd bet that she'd been watching their film; he'd left the tablet for her, after all, thinking that she could keep it.

"So are you just checking up on me?" she asked. "Making sure I'm still breathing after what you put me through?"

God, she sounded so lighthearted, and it nudged at him.

Words banged at him, as if he couldn't hold back the explanation he owed her. He wanted her to know that even though he'd left after what they'd shared, there was good reason.

He just didn't know how to start everything off, so, of course, he did it the wrong way.

"I heard about your sister."

"Oh. Gossip gets around the ranch fast, doesn't it?"

"It does." He didn't want her to mention her time with Adam, and she didn't.

What Leigh didn't know, though, was that it'd been the real Adam who'd heard her story and seen her reaction up close. While she'd talked about her sister, there'd been a sorrowful sheen in her eyes that she'd valiantly chased away, and he'd admired that, because he couldn't do it with Carla.

But it'd taken a lot for him to bring it up with Leigh right now, even though she was the only woman he'd dated that he could talk to about this.

"I had a wife," he said bluntly, ungracefully, but it felt

good to get it off his chest. He wanted her to know why he was the way he was, and it had nothing to do with her.

"You...*had* a wife?" she asked.

"A while ago." What was he trying to tell her? Could he even say more?

"What was she like—?" Leigh started to ask.

But that was all he had in him. "I'm only telling you this because I understand how it feels to dedicate yourself to someone you miss, just as you do with your show and your sister."

"You still dedicate yourself to your wife."

He nodded, but he realized that she couldn't see him. Not that it mattered, because she was a smart woman, and she would've already figured out his answer.

"That's okay," she said, her words rushed. Then she slowed down. "I mean, I figured there was someone."

"Why?"

"Callum. Let's be honest with each other. You didn't invite me on these dates to have a deep connection. I knew that. You wanted to...forget about something. I don't take it personally."

Really? Was that why he'd sensed a hurt in her? She had a right to it, too, with this warped version of afterglow pillow talk.

If he had any guts, he would've been talking to her about this as Adam, not Callum. The *real* Adam, too, and not a horse groom who worked on this estate.

The least he could do was be halfway honest with her. "You're right."

"I guess that's why you keep me around? Because I'm always right?"

There she went, lightening things up again. He found himself smiling. "You're good at coping, aren't you?"

"Maybe you could be, too."

He'd already proved that theory wrong over and over again, and he was sure he wouldn't be good at it anytime soon. Once these next few days were over, things would be the same as they always were.

"Callum?"

"Yes."

Her laugh was soft. "I thought you might've fallen asleep on me. It's getting late."

"Then I'll let you get back to bed."

"You mean, you don't want to—?" She cut herself off. "Okay."

It took him a moment to process what she'd almost asked him.

Was she thinking he was going to make his way over to her room again?

The raw truth hit him then: even if they'd just had a heartfelt conversation, she still saw him as one thing in the end. A playboy. A fun date. And she wanted to get back to it.

But had he said anything to make her think otherwise? And why the hell would he want her to believe there was a chance of anything else?

Disappointment gnashed at him, but he should've expected it. The bottom line was that Leigh had come on this trip for new experiences, not to hear him moping.

She obviously knew the conversation was over. "Sweet dreams," she said.

He wished her good-night, too, knowing that his dreams would be just as haunted as ever.

10

DANI HAD BIG plans for her day off, so when she stepped out of the shower that morning, she quickly toweled off, put on a robe and made a beeline for her closet.

She was going to go shopping for a wedding ring for Riley while he was working as an estate manager out of town. She'd been putting off the ring thing because she just couldn't find the perfect style for him. That was what she'd kept saying anyway...until she'd come to realize that she'd been lying to herself about that.

Cold feet. It was finally time to admit she had them. The ring had only been a symptom of her bigger problem, and thank God she'd come to terms with it these past few days.

Rifling through her clothes, she first bypassed the cosmopolitan blouses and skirts she'd recently bought that resembled Margot's wardrobe; her friend's brassy Around the Girl in Eighty Ways basket had inspired more than just sexual experimentation in Dani—she'd always admired how Margot looked, too. But she was done with that makeover phase now. And she'd even come around to the conclusion that her job at the catering company was a darn good one, and she was lucky to have it in these rough times. There'd be plenty of years ahead when she and Riley could explore other options.

Plenty of time.

She got to the other side of her closet, with the flowery-print dresses that had defined the sweet, innocent Dani she'd been, pastel shirts that had complemented her curly red hair back before she'd chopped it off in this sharp bob that didn't feel quite right anymore…

She choked up, and before she knew it, she was crying like a moron, clutching one of the old Dani dresses, pressing her face into the worn cotton. Out of nowhere, her dad's voice entered her mind from that ugly day five years ago when her parents had told her they had something important to talk to her about.

Your mom and I haven't been happy for a while, Dani—

Then Mom, breaking in. *We're getting a divorce, honey.*

From the way Mom had glanced at Dad, Dani had known there was a bigger explanation that they weren't giving her, and it wasn't until months later that Mom finally got around to the full truth—that Dad's attentions had strayed.

We grew out of each other, she'd said, holding back the tears…

Dani's cheeks were wet as she let go of the dress. It was all just hitting her now: she could buy new clothes, take a new job, be a strong woman in and out of the bedroom—and she would still do that—but there were some things she couldn't ever change.

Like who she really was.

Utterly helpless, she sat on the floor, her back to

the wall, crying about the anguish her mom had gone through, crying because anyone could get hurt, crying until she was out of tears.

Her wedding feet were freezing. When would she get ahold of herself?

She got up, reached for her phone on the nightstand and dialed a number. Leigh would understand her predicament more than love-happy Margot right now.

It didn't take but a couple of rings for her friend to answer.

"Help?" Dani asked with a semicroak.

"Dani? Are you okay?"

She thought she heard something clang on the other end of the line. "Yeah." A mistimed sob broke into her voice. "Are you cooking right now? I can call back."

"No, tell me what's wrong."

Without further ado, she told Leigh everything. Good heavens, she'd been holding it all back for a while now, pretending life was hunky-dory when fear and doubt had been tearing her up inside, even as she'd become more assertive in other ways. She told Leigh things she hadn't even told Riley about, like how she fully expected him to do her wrong in the future just as her dad had done to her mom, and how ridiculous she was being because Riley would never betray her.

Just as her mom had thought her dad wouldn't.

"All along I thought I was having an identity crisis, but that's not what was going on at all," she said. "I want to get over it, but I can't, and each day that passes makes me want to throw up, Leigh. How's that for a bride-to-be?"

"I'm sure this has happened to more than one woman." Leigh, so calm, so practical. "Can you tell Riley everything you told me, then take it from there? You'll feel way better."

"It'd be a slap in his face, especially since he thinks I've gotten over the hump. He'd wonder why I can't trust him when he's earned it. He'll think there's something wrong with him, not me, because that's just how he is—a man who takes everything on himself."

"A prince among men." Leigh's pause was a little too long.

"Leigh?" Dani asked, sniffling. "Is there something *you* should be telling *me*? Should we be commiserating together about your date or...?"

"Not at all. I'm having the best time."

So why did she sound *too* chipper?

"Listen," Leigh said, "I'm actually in the middle of cooking breakfast. Would it be okay if I called you later?"

"Definitely." Dani wiped her face. "I'm pretty sure I got the worst of it out of me anyway with this attractive spaz attack. And I really should get moving."

"Work?"

"No, I'm off to..." Oh, God, to buy Riley's ring. "Do errands."

"You're truly fine? You're not just saying that?"

Dani's gaze lingered on the old flowered dress that seemed so drab next to the more sophisticated new clothes. "Yes, I'm fine."

As they disconnected, Dani went to sit on her bed, slowly letting out her breath. The phone call really had helped; she was already feeling better. And any minute now her roiling stomach would receive the same message.

Any minute now.

LEIGH HUNG UP the phone and put it on the upper counter, away from the batter bowl and hodgepodge of ingredients she'd pulled out of the fridge and pantry for the lemon pancakes she'd decided to throw together.

Based on what she'd found in the fridge and pantry, she'd tossed a bit of lemon zest and juice into the white wheat-flour mix just to see where it all went.

Adventures in the kitchen. She'd awakened early following a night of tossing and turning after Callum had made that call to her. So as soon as she could, she'd come here, seeking comfort in what she did best. But her heart wasn't into cooking as much as it usually was, and it had nothing to do with Dani's situation, either—although that was definitely giving Leigh some concern.

Dani was obviously anxious about the wedding. Totally stressed out. And Leigh had already decided she would be making it a priority to de-stress the bride-to-be when this date was finished. Dani had a wedding-planning get-together this weekend anyway, and Lord help them all if she was still a mess at that point.

Leigh stopped stirring the batter to drink from the glass of orange juice that she'd squeezed with a juicer.

She couldn't help obsessing a little about where Callum was this morning, when he'd call. Couldn't she even go a few hours without him? All that'd been keeping her together was the film she'd watched more than a few times last night. But it wasn't the same as having him with her, where she could touch him, smell his skin, burrow against him for a short time.

God, she was hopelessly trapped in him and his games.

And she feared she was trapped in maybe even more

than just that. Because he had phoned her to lay his soul bare, and it'd gotten to her.

A wife, she thought for about the hundredth time. He was mourning a wife, and for some reason he'd felt compelled to let her know about that. The most moving thing about the call was how he'd sounded; it hadn't been self-assured like the Callum she'd come to know but…brokenhearted.

Yes, that was exactly what he'd been, and at that moment, his games had all made sense to her. Was he a man who couldn't handle anything serious, so he went for the opposite?

But just as they'd been getting somewhere with each other, she must've said something wrong, because he'd become guarded again, and they'd ended the call on a bad note. It was almost as if he were more of a stranger to her than ever, and she wasn't sure if he would even want to see her today. Or tomorrow.

Yet after his bombshell, she couldn't just assume that and abandon him. He'd grabbed her heart last night with that call, squeezing it, introducing emotion into a scenario that was never supposed to have any.

And it was such a bad idea for her to want to comfort him now, even though he'd started off doing just that to her during his phone call, telling her that he understood about losing someone. But it was only that… damn it, she'd started to feel something, and wanting to comfort him seemed natural. How dumb was that, though, if Callum was suffering from a torn-up heart? Talk about being in second place in life; she was just asking for it by getting in deeper with a man who still seemed to put another woman first.

A sinking sensation in her belly made her pause

in bringing the juice glass to her mouth for another drink, but when she realized what she was doing, she rebounded quickly, taking another sip. She couldn't let his moods affect her. Wouldn't.

When she heard boot steps on the tile, she glanced up to see Adam entering the kitchen area, his Stetson in his hands, his black hair mussed once again.

She imagined herself reaching up to smooth it back in place, her stomach flipping.

Great. Could she be a bigger bundle of hormones? She was just projecting onto the nearest hot guy because now that Callum had sexed her up, she needed more, and Adam was available.

"Mornin'," the cowboy said, stopping by the counter where Leigh was taking slices of bacon out of the package and readying the skillet.

"Morning," Leigh echoed. His drawl struck her again with how un-Callum-like it was. "You here early to pick me up for my ride with Bessie Blue?"

At the excitement in her tone, he smiled, and she looked away. Maybe she and Bessie would have a talk today about men.

"Not necessarily," he said. "Don't think I'm presumptuous, but I told a neighbor about you and your show, and he wondered if he could do some breakfast sampling. Mrs. Ellison said you were in here cooking up a storm."

"I'm humbled that you all would want anything that I make." She smiled, laying the bacon down to fry. Then she poured a glass of juice for him as he took a seat at the counter, as if he wanted a front-row view for the culinary show Leigh was putting on while he waited for the pancakes.

Just don't look at him and you'll be okay, she told

herself as he drank. And the strategy worked…at least for the time it took to fry that bacon.

When she was done, she took the bacon off to drain on paper towels. *No projecting. No warming up to Adam just because Callum's giving you a tough time.*

Adam cleared his throat, but when she glanced at him, he was looking away from her as he usually did, as if he didn't want her to catch him checking her out. A flutter twirled up her chest at the thought.

Stop.

"Lemon pancakes?" he asked. "Is that what you're making?"

She pointed to the yellow fruit peels on the counter, nodding, and he laughed.

"I know—good guess. I can't say I've ever had any."

Scooping the refuse from the counter and tossing it in the nearby garbage basket, she said, "I found some lemons and all the basics around, so I just went for it, even though it's way more decadent than my usual breakfast." She was going to be careful about falling into old habits, eating when she got frustrated about something or another. Mainly, she'd cooked for Callum this morning, hoping he would show up at some point.

She shrugged. "Anyway, it looks like someone stocked this kitchen well."

"Mrs. Ellison went to a nearby farm stand early this morning." Adam picked up his glass again. "It's her usual routine."

After he drank, he put his glass down, then smoothed back his hair. He was sitting half on, half off his stool, as if he couldn't decide if he was staying or going. It seemed that he was being extremely watchful with her, assessing her, and she was pretty sure why that was.

She laughed. "You act like you're afraid I'll start grilling you again about Callum. Don't worry yourself about it."

It was as if she'd called him out, and he relaxed, finally hanging his hat and on the back of the neighboring barstool. "I'm safe, then?"

Callum would've already turned this into a sparring match. Adam's disposition was the polar opposite.

"You're safe." She patted the bacon dry. "But that doesn't mean I can't ask about you, right?"

He leaned forward, resting his arms on the counter. "I guess you can try."

"Okay. You don't sound like a SoCal native. Too much of a drawl in your voice."

"Then I guess I'll have to tone it down."

"That was kind of my way of asking where you're really from."

"Here, there." He furrowed his brow. "Maybe that's where I picked up the accent."

"That answer sure covers all the bases."

After a beat he pushed away his glass. "My family had a ranch in central California a long time ago. I sold it off when they passed on, made my way around, then ended up here."

See, a little tenacity always paid off. Just when she'd started to think that she wasn't going to meet any more nonevasive guys in her lifetime, Adam had come through with an actual answer about himself. He seemed more comfortable now, too, and that made her feel the same. She even got the hankering to get a little feisty with her cooking, and she decided to veer from the recipe she'd settled on in her head, chopping up the bacon and putting it into the batter instead of serving it on the side.

Then she heated the griddle for the pancakes, adding butter to the surface.

"*Bacon*-and-lemon pancakes?" he asked.

"I'm feeling deviant." Then she used the same term Callum had back at the first mansion when they'd talked about her cooking habits. "I'm trying a little freestyling."

Adam paused, then sat back in his stool, running a hand over his chin. "Glad to be here for the big event."

She poured dollops of batter onto the griddle, standing by with the spatula and a large plate. The aroma of the food added a homey atmosphere to the kitchen, and she was enjoying Adam's quiet presence. When was the last time she'd felt that way around someone?

"So," she said, "taking up where you conveniently left off with your life's story…"

"I was hoping you'd forget what we were talking about."

She motioned toward herself with the spatula, then started to flip the pancakes. "I'm persistent. At least, I've been told."

"What else do you want to know, then?"

"How about your job? Do you like it?"

"My job." He made eye contact with her, his gaze gold. "It passes the days."

"You'd rather be doing something else?" she asked, not thinking about his eyes. Not remotely.

He laughed softly. "Well, I haven't thought about job options in a long time, Miss Leigh."

"It's just Leigh."

As they looked at each other a beat too long—she, trying to figure out what was going on with herself, he, affable but somehow unreadable—Leigh shut off the griddle, transferring the pancakes to the main plate.

She wasn't sure what it was about Adam, but she felt as if they'd fallen into some kind of immediately friendly groove—that he was a kind of neutral comfort zone for her as they lingered in the kitchen together.

She'd already gotten the bottle of maple syrup out of the cupboard, and not seeing the sense in fancying it up by putting it into a small serving pitcher, she set it on the counter in front of him.

After placing a couple plates there, too, she said, "Load up before I cook up more for your neighbor friend."

He took a few pancakes but didn't make a move to go to the small nook table, so she decided there was no harm in eating where they were. Besides, being at the table with him alone seemed like…well, a date or something.

"Oh, damn," he said after taking a bite. "No wonder you're a star."

She started to wave off the compliment but then thought of what Callum had said about how she reacted to praise. So she accepted this one with grace.

"Thank you."

"I should be thanking you."

They ate a few bites until she realized that he'd come to survey her again. Enough was enough.

"What?" she asked. "Have I had something on my face the last twenty hours?"

He seemed to realize what he was doing, then stuck his fork into his food. "It's nothing. I just can't help wondering…"

"Out with it, please."

Grinning, he gave in. "It's Callum."

"Okay."

"There're a few rumors about him being...different. I mean, I've met the man, but..."

"There are rumors?"

So who was asking the tough questions now? But she'd been hoping for someone to talk to, and maybe Adam knew something about Callum, even "through the grapevine."

Leigh glanced around the huge kitchen, then lowered her voice so even a listening device would have a hard time picking up her words, if Callum had gone high-tech and even stranger on her.

"Go on," she said.

"I'm just kind of curious what you think of him."

She hadn't anticipated a question like that, and the first thing that ran through her head was, *I'm in second place.*

His wife. He'd told her that he still missed her, still dedicated himself to her. And no matter how Leigh had started to feel about him and how far they'd gone last night, that was all that mattered.

"What do I think?" she repeated, only now attempting to recover, smiling while chasing off the heart-grasping feelings that had rolled over her. "He's the best host a girl could ask for."

Adam's golden, penetrating gaze went a little distant, and at first she thought it was because she sounded so flippant, and maybe even cheap. What else would a cowboy like him think about a woman who was only here for sex? If he even knew what she was here for.

He got up from his stool, grabbing his hat and pushing it onto his head until the brim hid his face. His shoulders were tight, his stance almost awkward.

"That was an intrusive question I shouldn't have

asked," he said, heading for the exit. "Forget I said anything."

Now she was utterly bewildered, not only by the feelings his question had evoked but by his behavior. *Did* he think she was a slut and he didn't want to hear about it?

"Adam," she said, calling after him. "The pancakes…"

But he was already gone.

"I SHOULDN'T HAVE been surprised at her answer."

Adam was in his rented pickup, miles down the road, his cell phone on the dashboard as he talked to Beth. The taste of lemon, bacon and maple syrup still lingered in his mouth.

A random thought rose up among all the others: Leigh had been freestyling with her food this morning. Hadn't she told him she always played it safe? Somehow he'd believed that reflected a change in her—a sign that she had let go of all her hang-ups and had opened herself up more than usual. Spurred on by the thought of what else she might've opened herself up to, "Adam" had asked her what she thought of Callum, giving her an opportunity to say…something. Anything that would give him an idea of… What? If she was feeling something for him?

Why had a tiny flicker of hope inside of him been longing for another sign from her that there was more to the two of them than just sex?

Remorse filled him just as much as a sense of betrayal where Carla was concerned. But there was also a shocking disappointment in the answer he'd actually gotten from Leigh.

"Isn't this what you wanted?" Beth asked on the other

end of the phone from her home up in Cambria. This morning an urgent board meeting had come up for the day after tomorrow, so she'd been taking care of out-of-state travel arrangements for him. He hadn't been able to stop himself from pouring this out to her, though.

"Yes," he said. "I'm getting everything I set out to get from her." So why did it all feel so empty?

The thought wounded him, a self-inflicted injury, because neither of them was supposed to care. Or maybe it was just Carla's ghostly voice beating him up from the inside out. *Didn't you tell me that I would be the only one, forever...?*

She'd never said those words to him in real life. It was merely his guilt talking. So why did it always sound so real?

Unfortunately, guilt was what ruled him because, for the first time, he'd been beyond attracted to a woman who wasn't his wife. He'd never been so confused, hating himself for the wrenching sense of disloyalty that pressed down on him.

He'd played his games, all right, trying to fulfill the needs of his body while keeping his emotions out of it. He'd been so sure he'd held a winning hand the whole time that it stunned him to be trumped by his own feelings.

Beth had been restraining herself from offering any opinions, but he knew what she wanted to say.

"You told me so," he whispered. "Go ahead, give it to me."

"No." Her voice was thick. "I'm not going to add to what we both know will come next with you."

The dark mood.

"I can tell you're already worse than usual," she said.

"Why don't you say what you're honestly feeling, Adam? Tell me that you're falling for her."

"I haven't. I won't." He could turn all his emotions off again, just as he'd done when "cowboy Adam" had heard Leigh's casual comment about what Callum meant to her.

"Adam," Beth said. "Goddamn it, when're you going to finally get over this?"

"Are you talking about mourning Carla?"

"Yes. Because it can't go on forever."

But he'd promised Carla forever.

By her bedside, holding her frail hand, a weak smile on her face as he tried not to hold too hard. She obviously knew she was about to go, that she was seeing him for the last time, and she'd been attempting not to cry.

Still, there was a tear that didn't know any better, and it slid down her cheek, tearing him apart.

"Adam…"

As her voice faded off, he thought of never hearing her say his name again, and he pressed her hand to his cheek. His own wet cheek. He wanted her to know that he would always be hers, wanted her to leave him feeling loved.

"I promise you, Carla, you'll be the only one I'll love. Stay with me a little longer, though, okay? Don't make me think about things like that until…"

But she'd already left him, and as the serrated memory knifed him now, even though she'd never made him promise such a thing, he knew that he could never go through the pain of loss again with anyone. So, really, Leigh had done him a favor by letting "Adam" know what Callum really was to her. Leigh was a sweet, compassionate woman, but that was where it ended.

And that was a good thing.

So why was he sitting here in the darkest mood he'd ever experienced since Carla had died? "Adam?" Beth's voice. "Did you hear me? The mourning can't continue."

He gripped the steering wheel. It wasn't as if *Leigh* was insisting that he put a stop to his mourning. She was content with the status quo.

A part of his heart seemed to crack off and fall. He should be happy with what he had. Why couldn't he be?

The more he thought about it, the more he knew that what he'd done as Callum was the right way to go. No hurt, no pain, no emotions.

He would be the ultimate host, if that was what Leigh wanted.

"So what're you going to do?" Beth asked.

"Do?" He swallowed. "I'm going to continue this date. That's what she wants, and so do I."

"I just don't know what to say to you." It sounded as if Beth had a lump in her throat, too. "Go ahead. Do what you want. Continue wallowing in your grief and self-destructing. Go on lying to yourself, Adam, and maybe you'll miraculously feel better in the morning."

"Maybe I will."

As they finished their conversation, he told himself that he didn't need to feel anyway. Feelings were weakness. Feelings killed.

He dialed another number, and when Leigh answered, he had to remind himself that he was Callum the game player and no one else.

11

CALLUM HAD TOLD Leigh to meet him in one hour in the same room they'd been in yesterday. And he'd made one more request.

"When you go in there, choose any outfit you want from the armoire, then wait for me with the blindfold on. I'll call you."

Again with the blindfold. He was really determined to keep this secrecy thing going. It wasn't that she was discouraged by that, it was just…

Duh, Leigh, he all but told you why he does what he does. You don't have a shot in hell of getting into his heart, because it still belongs to his wife. Just take what he's offering for what it is—the best sex you've ever had.

But was devotion to his wife also the reason he hadn't stayed with Leigh last night after the sex? Because cuddling and real intimacy were things he'd saved for one woman and one alone?

As Leigh went to the appointed room, she couldn't get over how sad that was…and yet so romantic. *She'd* never had a man feel that strongly about her, and the fact

that Callum had once loved someone that much touched
Leigh in a way that nothing in their games ever could.

She opened the door, then closed it behind her, glancing at the other door in the wall. She'd sworn Callum
had been waiting behind it yesterday when she'd first
arrived, before she'd put on the blindfold. When she
looked around now, she could tell he'd already been in
here, because there was music playing from an iPod
dock on the mahogany nightstand.

No Johnny Cash this time; instead, a country-noir
song was whispering to her with a moody lady sing-
ing over a sexy guitar and light percussion with some
fiddle lingering in the background. The scent of leather
haunted the air, as if Callum had left that behind, too.

The cream blindfold she'd used yesterday afternoon
waited on the bed just like last time, but she went to the
armoire first. When she opened it, she found the silky
clothing and suits she'd discovered last time, but she
hadn't gotten to the far side of the wardrobe.

At the sight of the glamorous black-and-white gown
hanging there, she pulled in a breath. She took the dress
out, and the chiffon skirt tumbled to the carpet. On the
bodice, dark beaded swirls decorated the snowy material, but it was the back of the gown that captured her:
two black straps crisscrossing, ending up in a big chiffon bow.

Movie stars from the '40s had worn this kind of dress,
and it blew her away that Callum thought this suited
her. Then again, he'd always showered her with compliments, even if they'd only been a way to seduce her.

But the whole time, he had you in second place, she
thought again.

After grabbing a pair of strappy pumps from the bottom of the armoire, she went to the bed and pushed aside the mosquito netting, laying the gown on the mattress and doffing her shirt, jeans and undergarments, then slipping into the chiffon. When she had the shoes on, too, she undid her hair from the low ponytail she'd been wearing and went to the full-length mirror.

She looked like another woman entirely, but still the same Leigh Vaughn who'd finally become what she'd always dreamed of, even though her transformation was just as temporary as this thing with Callum was.

Pensively, she smoothed down her hair so that it fell over her shoulder in a sultry wave. The only thing wrong with this image was her expression. The sadness in her eyes. It was a reflection that showed the real her—a woman who'd gotten in too deep, her heart already aching at the thought that the game wouldn't mean as much to Callum as it did to her.

But why did sex all of a sudden have to mean love? Or at least the possibility of it? Wasn't she overjoyed at what Callum made her feel sexually? Wasn't she still addicted?

You're sad because this is happening with someone you've started to fall for, she thought.

The disposable phone she'd brought with her rang, and when she answered it, a zing electrified her through and through as she heard Callum's voice.

"Are you ready for me?"

Her heart crumbled. "Give me a minute. Then I'm all yours."

She wanted to cringe at the way she'd phrased that. She might be all his, but he still belonged to someone else.

"Let me know when you're ready," he said.

"I will."

Putting the phone on the bed, she sat between the parted mosquito netting, then picked up the blindfold and tied it at the back of her head. Total darkness; she was getting all too used to it.

She picked up the phone. "Ready now." Her pulse nearly blocked her throat. She would've been ready for so much more had he just said the word. But it was what it was, and she was going to have a great time. She would do just about anything for him, because he hadn't steered her wrong yet.

She heard a sound from across the bedroom, the door to the adjoining room opening, and her breath jammed in her lungs as she shut off and put down the phone.

Footsteps, anticipation, her heart jumping with each thud. And it was jumping so hard, crashing into her ribs, that it felt bruised.

Why had all her feelings come to the surface now, making things so clear to her at the wrong time? Was it because he was here in person? Here but not truly here?

She felt him standing in front of her, and her mind went fuzzy, her body a field of static. And when she felt him touching her hand, lifting it and helping her stand, shivers ran through her with such harsh speed that she could barely function.

But it was the kiss on the back of her hand that made her gasp.

The shape of his lips buzzed on her skin as he kept holding her. "You've surpassed every one of my fantasies," he said in that deep, smooth voice.

"I do my best," she said, trying to joke. "Fantasies'R'Me."

Although he chuckled, the quip still fell flat between them, but when his hands rubbed up and down her arms, then traveled to her nearly bare back, she didn't care about judging her sense of humor. She only floated in sensation, erotic and steamy.

"Do you trust me?" he asked again.

With the sex? Yes. But not with anything else.

"You know I do."

"That's the girl I know. You're a good player, Leigh," he said, and she could hear that he had a smile on his mouth. But the smile sounded tighter than usual. "You're all about the adventure, and you've always understood what makes me happy while making you happy."

Where was he going with this? It didn't sound as if he had another "guess where the feather's going to touch you" game in mind.

"That's right," she finally answered. "I'm all about the fun."

She thought she felt his hands stiffen on her back before he took them away.

"As you like it," he said.

Was there a note of something in his voice that she hadn't heard during any other personal encounter? It was as if he'd wanted her to say something else, but what?

"In one minute," he said, "I want you to take off that blindfold. Don't ask what you're going to see, because I'm not going to tell you."

He was having her take the mask all the way off? Now she was really intrigued. "All right."

In spite of her doubts about him, she thought that this could be it—the moment. The big reveal. Excitement took her over, and she got ready to doff the blindfold after the sixty seconds he'd requested.

When she heard the adjoining door shut, the excitement eased off. "Callum?" she asked.

No answer, but he'd done stuff like this before, so she counted down from sixty…to fifty…

She rushed to get to zero, and when she did, her hands trembled as they went for the blindfold, her fingers like wet noodles as she tried to work off the material.

When she was finally able to toss it away, she eagerly looked toward the door, finding nothing.

Until she felt someone standing near the window.

She turned her gaze there, her mind scrambling at who she saw in his usual plaid shirt and a pair of jeans, hooking his thumbs into his belt loops like the cowboy he was.

ADAM DIDN'T KNOW what to do when Leigh took off that blindfold and just stared at him.

While she'd been counting down the minute, Adam had pretended he was leaving the room, then sneaked softly over to the window. Not knowing what to do next, he'd merely fisted his hands by his sides. It was only at the last few seconds, when she was struggling to take off the blindfold, that he'd decided to appear more casual. That was because she didn't care about anything other than sex, either, and all they were here for was to push the physical limits with each other, just as they'd always done. Right?

Adrenaline shredded his veins as she just kept staring at him. But when she glanced at the door where Callum had supposedly disappeared, he knew that she wasn't just taken off guard. There was a glow in her gaze that told him she was considering what Callum had suggested, that she was so caught up in these fantasies that she couldn't put the brakes on.

But there was confusion in her gaze, too.

Being careful to use his "Adam" drawl, he spoke before she could. "You're wondering why I'm here."

"I think I have an idea."

He had a story all worked up—a fiction that would keep the fun going while never letting her know exactly who he was. Neither of them would have any reason to contact each other after the date anyway. They would both just move on as he'd always intended, so no harm, no foul by tossing out a few more white lies.

"Callum's in the other room," he said. "Listening, watching."

"How's he watching us?"

"He's got more money than he knows what to do with, so there're ways. Believe me."

She gazed around the room, probably searching for camouflaged cameras. But she liked cameras—that had been established yesterday. She'd had a sexual awakening he'd initiated within her, and she was probably dreaming of bodies entangled, adventures and fantasies unwound.

"A threesome," she said softly. "Not a traditional one, but you're in here, I'm in here and Callum's watching. That makes three of us."

"You could call it that."

As Adam attempted to read her, he realized that he hadn't just wanted to see what her reaction would be to finding "Adam" in the room. He was testing her until she wouldn't be able to take any more. Actually, he even wanted her to be the one who dismissed Callum instead of him dismissing her.

But he had started this, and he couldn't be stung if she wanted to go through with it.

"How did you get recruited for this?" she asked. "Is it the first time or is it part of the job description?"

Ouch. But in answer, he let down his shields for once—and once only—allowing all the desire he had for her to shine through his gaze.

Her lips parted as if she got his message loud and clear.

Was it possible that she was holding back an attraction to Adam?

"You don't know much about me," he said. "But I've never been able to say no to a beautiful woman, and when Callum suggested I come up here, I sure as hell didn't say no."

When she didn't respond, a tiny spark flitted through him. The thought of being with her, face-to-face, thrilled him. She would never know that he and Callum were the same person; it would be the ultimate game.

But it wasn't sitting right with him, and he hated himself more than ever now for not leaving well enough alone, for leaving himself open to getting flayed by all the emotions swooping down on him.

Pushing back his hair from his face, he sent a lowered look to her, and she absently rubbed her hands up and down her arms, as if this scenario gave her goose bumps. He yearned to do the same thing to her, remembering the feel of her skin just a few minutes ago when "Callum" had been in here.

"All Callum wants," Adam said, "is to watch your face when you're at your happiest."

"Creative guy, isn't he?" She looked at the door again, then back at Adam. "If he was the one in here with me, he wouldn't be able to see all of my face because I'd have a blindfold over my eyes. But with you, he's free to sit back in the other room and enjoy while your hands take the place of his. It's almost like a film, only he's the one who gets to watch it."

What she didn't know was that this would be the last time between them. Adam had to make sure of it because, even now, it felt as if his heart was breaking.

But he'd asked her to do this. Callum had.

She laughed a bit. "So Callum likes to watch."

That's not all I can do, Adam thought.

She looked at the door again, then turned toward him, taking a step forward.

Adam's body took over, physical sensations eclipsing everything in his mind, but his heart was still in limbo, hovering, waiting for her next step.

A THREESOME, LEIGH THOUGHT. She'd never in her wildest dreams believed she would even be considering it.

Why *not* jump all the way into this? Callum wanted it.

Her body said *yesyesyes, please continue.* This was just another way to explore the sexuality that'd been pressed into her and hidden for so long, and no one could take it away from her now that it'd emerged.

Yet before she could take another step, Adam came toward her, and she stopped.

"The first moment I saw you, Leigh," he said in that sexy drawl, "I wanted this."

There was such an intensity about him that she couldn't go on. She'd always longed for someone to say something like that to her, but that wasn't the real reason her skin was tingling. The way Adam had uttered it told her that he wasn't putting her on or merely trying to get into her figurative pants. He truly meant it.

She allowed herself to really appreciate him for the first time: his glossy, thick black hair, his tanned skin, his compelling gold eyes that gleamed like a predator that knew what would appease its hunger. He was built strong, with wide shoulders, muscled arms, and she could imagine what they would feel like wrapped around her.

But she also wanted Callum's arms. Damn him. Why did her thoughts always go back to him?

Adam spoke. "I only want to touch you, make you feel good."

"Just like Callum." She was dwelling on the "touch you" part. Did that mean they weren't going to go all the way?

With a sidelong glance, she looked toward the door again. She couldn't stop it. Was Callum in the other room, enjoying the show?

Adam came to her, such a tender expression on his face that she blinked. He'd been hiding his attraction to her, just as Callum always hid. It was only now, when he had permission to show it, that his need for her was clear.

Reaching her, he lifted his hand, resting it on her bare shoulder, then tracing it down her arm, leaving a trail of raised hairs and awakened skin.

Her breathing had turned erratic, even with this one minor gesture. And when he skimmed his fingertips back up her arm, his gaze was muddy, as if he was struggling for control.

"Is it okay for me to go on?" he asked, the same way Callum had always sought her permission.

She thought of Callum in the next room, watching, waiting.

Before she could answer, Adam did something totally unexpected. As the country-noir music played on, just as if they were in a darkened club in the middle of a night-washed nowhere, he pulled her to him, grasping her hand and bringing it to his shoulder.

He began to lead her in a slow, breath-stealing dance, her chest to his, her heartbeat pounding against him.

"Leigh," he whispered, as if trying out her name, seeing if it belonged to him or not.

It didn't, but something inside her sure wanted it to in this crazy moment. Callum had been seductive but never this romantic. It was as if she had one side of a coin sitting in the other room while the second side was here, leading her in a surprisingly sweet dance.

A bass plucked away on the sound track, complementing the singer's soulful voice.

His cheek was against her head. "I like when you wear your hair down," he said.

True—it had always been in a braid or ponytail around him. But how many times had he seen her?

He put a stop to her curiosity when he slid his hand to the small of her exposed back, just above the expansive bow of her gown. Stroking there, he kept swaying with her.

It was all a dream: like Callum, he smelled of leather, but the outside kind, not from fancy furniture inside a beautiful house. Most important, though, Adam was willing to show his face, revealing his soul in his eyes.

When he dragged his fingertips up the center of her back, following the bumps of her spine, she stopped dancing, thinking about Callum watching.

This is what he asked for, she thought. So she let Adam draw his fingers over other parts of her back, high and low, slow and sensual.

"You're everything I ever thought you'd be," he whispered near her ear.

Strange, the way he'd said it, as if the first time he'd seen her in those stables had really marked him. But when he brought his hands to her face, cupping it, looking into her eyes, she got too lost to think anymore.

Passion-dizzy persuasion—that was what filled Adam's gaze, and it made her chest cave in under a melting warmth.

But when he lowered his mouth to hers, she swerved away from him.

Cheating, she thought. This felt just like cheating, and it wasn't right at all.

He pulled back slightly, his fingers encircling her upper arms like the silken cords Callum had used. "Leigh, is the answer yes or no...?" he asked, clearly surprised at her response.

Maybe that was why his accent had disappeared.

Leigh froze, because his voice... Oh, my God, his *voice.*

When he froze, too, she stared up at him, backing away.

Had she heard what she thought she'd heard?

"Callum?" she asked.

12

SHIT.

Maybe he should've used the dramatic chops he'd developed lately to throw her off track—*what're you talking about, darlin'? I'm just some cowboy, not the demented rich guy in the next room*—but he knew his face confessed everything.

He was Callum…sort of. And the charade was over.

As he held up his hands in guilty surrender, his groin agonized with all the pounding blood there. But it was his chest that was paining him the most, as if something were twisting and trying to bend toward her.

She was leveling an injured look at him, backing away so that a chasm opened between them. "Damn it, say something. Who are you?"

The answer wasn't as easy as she might've been imagining. "I'm Callum…and Adam."

"Stop messing with me."

Last week, when this had all started, he might've taken her anger in stride, but he couldn't now. If she walked out that door, he wasn't sure what he would do.

Yet if she stayed, would that be equally as bad for him?

It seemed she'd reached her boiling point, and she headed for the exit.

"Don't go," he said in his natural voice—no drawl, no pretense. "Please, Leigh."

His last two words kept her in place, her back to him. "Why should I stay?" she said softly.

Because he wanted her to hear him out? Odd, but this moment was actually bigger than if he'd walked in here from the other room, revealing what he looked like. This unmasking was scarier—the unveiling of what he was like inside.

He still wasn't sure he was ready to let go of his biggest obstacle to getting close to Leigh, though. A tug of war raged inside him—*just let Leigh go.... No, make her stay*—and she sighed, looking so out of place in that fantasy dress. This was reality now, so it didn't belong anymore.

When he said nothing, she went for the door again. "Whatever, Callum."

Emotions burst out of him, seizing him. "Adam," he said. "My name is Adam."

That halted her for good, and since she was still on one side of the room and he was on the other, it seemed so much easier to explain everything to her now that he didn't have to look in her eyes.

She turned her head only slightly but he could tell she was glaring at him. "Adam...what?"

"Adam Morgan." As soon as he said his full name, it felt as if a ten-ton boulder had been lifted off his shoulders.

He could see that she was running the name through

her mind, sifting through memories in an attempt to find him. But she obviously came up blank.

"You wouldn't know me," he said. "We didn't even officially meet. I was a freshman at Cal-U when you were, and we were both pledging our sorority and fraternity when I saw you at a party. It was at Gary Ballard's house." Gary had been a junior, and all the underclassmen had felt like hot shit partying with him.

"One party ran into the other back then," she said, turning around a little more but not much. Just enough so that some of her hair shimmered down her shoulder with the movement, falling over part of her exposed back. "I never met you, but you remembered me enough to bid on my basket at the auction?"

"That's half the story." Now that the dam was broken, this was so much simpler. But it felt as if it was too late all the same.

To think he'd been hoping for a chance like this—one that would allow him to easily break off whatever they had going. One that would give her an excuse to leave him all on her own. But then he'd danced with her, and the world had spun. It was true that a twinge of betrayal still held him back from pouring out everything to her, yet getting Leigh to stay seemed more important than his guilt about Carla for now.

She shook her head. "I still don't understand. Why didn't I meet you at any of the functions or charity events our sorority and fraternity had together?"

"I left school not long into the first semester," he said. "My dad died, and I was the oldest in the family, so I went home to help my mom raise my sister and two brothers. Mom needed all the help she could get."

By now Leigh had come to face him. "That's awful."

He nodded, needing to move forward. He only wished it could be that easy with Carla, too, but the scars he carried from her were newer, fresher.

Yet Leigh was right here, and he just couldn't let her go. "Years later," he said, "I hired Beth as my right-hand woman, and she still kept in touch with everyone in the sorority. She told me about the reunion and who was putting the basket auction together."

"Margot and I," Leigh said. "That's when you remembered me?"

"Yes." He almost looked away from her, as he'd been doing so much in his Adam identity. But this time, he took the chance of seeing if her heart was in her eyes, as he suspected his own might be.

She was staring at the ground; she was the one who was hiding now. "So you're saying that you remembered me from one little college party, and you sent Beth to bid on my basket so you could have a date with me."

"I'd seen you on TV, and it reminded me of…" God, should he lay it all out?

Yes. Damn it, *yes.*

"It reminded me of how I had an across-the-room crush on you all those years ago, even if I didn't know you. If I'd stayed in school, maybe I would've eventually introduced myself, but I was kind of shy back then anyway, so who knows."

"You're not so shy these days."

"Neither are you." He thought of how she'd almost taken part in the so-called threesome. But he wouldn't blame her; after all, "Callum" had given her permission to be with Adam.

Instead of blushing, Leigh was looking straight at

him, and the eye contact made him simmer inside. It only took a look from her.

But his sense of betraying Carla rose up like a wave gathering strength, and he was barely able to shove it away.

She shook her head again. "Under normal circumstances, I'd say that's a romantic story you just gave me. I should be flattered."

"But this has gone beyond normal."

He suspected she wanted to know more about Carla, and her expectant gaze confirmed that.

"I haven't exactly gotten out since my wife died," he said. "I haven't been…ready. So when I asked Beth to bid on your basket, I already knew that we weren't going to have a run-of-the-mill date. I'm a businessman who makes deals on real estate and start-up companies all the time, but…" This was mortifying.

"Go on," she said.

Her voice, soft and gentle, gave him the strength to continue. "I'm used to online computer relationships. Or more like nonrelationships."

"You always have a distance between you and women?"

"Since Carla died, yes."

Was she going to think he was less of a man because of it? No, from the way she was watching him, she thought he was more of one for admitting it.

So he went on. "I really did intend for that date to be one night only, a silly, fun time together, and that would be that. I just wanted to complete my youthful fantasy of going out with you, and nothing more."

"But then you asked me to come back."

"And you did."

She hesitated, then said, "I thought I felt a… I don't know. A *connection* might be the wrong word, seeing as it didn't turn out to be one, after all."

Wham—a bull's-eye hit. So she really didn't feel a connection with him, even after he'd put himself out there to explain?

When she crossed her arms over her chest as if protecting herself, he wasn't sure about that. Was she hiding what she really felt? Or was that too much to hope?

She spoke again. "It's so clear to me that you refuse to have a connection, Adam. You told me just as much last night when you let me know about your wife."

"Carla." Now he crossed his arms, too. "I didn't tell you the details, though. She died two years ago of breast cancer."

"I'm so sorry." She paused. "It's as if she's still with you."

He felt the pressure of that boulder coming down on him again, pushing him back into a dark corner. "I told her I would never forget her, but you know that already."

"Yes."

They merely stood there, everything out in the open between them except for how they felt here and now. He should say something more, but he wasn't sure what. After all, he'd just told her once again that Carla was still a part of his life. What was Leigh supposed to do with that?

She held up her hands, then took a step backward. "I guess that's all there is to it, then."

"Leigh…"

She stopped. "What? What do you want me to do? Should I put a blindfold on so I don't have to see how you still feel about Carla?"

His shoulders sank. She was right. What exactly did he want from Leigh? Sex wasn't enough, but he didn't have the guts to come out of the shadows in any other way.

She laughed, a wounded sound. "All my life I've never been first with anyone. Not with my parents. Not with boys. Not even with anything I've ever accomplished. And now that I'm standing here with you, I realize that I need someone who'll give me the respect I deserve. I'm not saying a man should ever forget about the woman he loved and lost, but to put her memory above the person who's standing before him, wanting to lay out her heart…?"

As she wiped at her face, her words rang in his ears.

She was waiting for him to tell her that he was going to change, wasn't she? But he couldn't do that, and she gathered her dress in her hands, heading for the door, abandoning him. The storm of emotions hit him with such brutality that he couldn't do anything but stand there and brace himself.

Keeping him from going after the only woman who'd made him feel since his wife's death.

HE'D KNOWN LEIGH would leave right after their confrontation, and once arrangements had been made to schedule an earlier flight and get her to the airport, Adam had watched her go from an upper story window.

Watching once again.

And as she'd gotten into the limo in front of the house, he knew where she was going—to her friend Dani's house, then Margot's, where she and Leigh would be having a wedding-planning party. Leigh had mentioned this to Beth when his assistant had booked the transportation, but it didn't matter where she'd be.

She wasn't going to be here.

Before she'd gotten all the way into the limo, she'd turned around once as if knowing just where he was waiting and had given him a long, regretful look.

He'd touched the window, wanting to call out to her at the last minute, but what would he have said? Nothing. They were at an impasse—Leigh needing one thing, Adam not able to give it over.

But as the rest of the day passed, then the next and another, the hole in Adam's chest only got bigger. And there was no doubt it was because he'd thrown away the sort of chance most people lived a lifetime hoping for.

Now, on his home estate in Cambria after a business trip during which he'd basically sleepwalked his way through board meetings, he left his suitcase unpacked and went to his bedroom. There he opened a dresser drawer where a silk-swathed package waited. He'd been doing so much thinking during his trip, and he'd come to a firm conclusion.

He couldn't put off this moment any longer.

After undoing the material from around the item, he merely stared at the silver jewelry box with a carousel horse etched into the lid. He'd special-ordered it to commemorate the day he'd asked Carla to marry him, and she'd kept her favorite pearl necklace in here.

If he were to open the box, he'd see only her ashes now.

He went to sit down on the bed, just holding her, sadness closing his throat.

All the thinking he'd been doing since Leigh had left

finally clarified in that one moment, just as if a box inside of him had been opened.

Carla would've wanted him to be happy, and he'd been doing his best to make sure it didn't happen. He'd been making excuse after excuse, but they just weren't working anymore. Not since Leigh had come into his life....

Beth eventually wandered into his room with some contracts he needed to sign, putting them aside. She sat next to him, clearly recognizing the box.

He spoke without preamble. "In those last few minutes with Carla, I made a promise." He ran his finger over the carousel horse. "I always thought I'd be able to keep it."

"I know, Adam."

And the next time he'd looked, she'd been gone.

Beth rested her hand on his arm. There'd been days when she had hinted around this subject before, and he'd been too destroyed emotionally to hear what she had to say. But she'd known, and it was different now. He was ready to hear her talk about what *he* already knew.

She continued, sounding relieved that he was finally coming around to having this conversation. "Carla was my friend, too, and I know for a fact she wanted you to be happy. She wasn't selfish enough to think that you'd never fall in love again, and she would've been heartbroken to see you like this."

"It's just hard to let her go."

"You don't have to. But you can't use her as an excuse to pull away from what's inside of you, either."

When he heard Beth catch a quick breath, he realized she was trying to hold back a sob. He looked at her, and her eyes were filled with tears.

He'd never meant to bring anyone pain, and he knew that his best friend couldn't help but feel it whenever she looked at him. And as for Leigh…?

Gripping the box, he wasn't sure if she might be thinking of him, too. Did she still want to lay her heart out to him, as she'd said before she left?

He reached over and wiped Beth's cheeks with his thumb, then rested his head against hers.

"Please don't fade away before your time just like Carla did," she said. "Promise *me*, Adam."

Unable to speak, he let her go then, the room so quiet that he could hear the wind through the pines outside.

It was almost as if he could pick out Carla's whispers through the trees. He and she had bought this place before she'd died, but they'd never had the chance to move in. She'd loved the Colonial-style house, the pines, and he'd described them to her sometimes on her bad days when the sickness had racked her. The image of trees had never failed to cheer her up.

He got up from the bed, taking the box with him as he left the room. He went outside to the porch, then walked farther, into the midst of the pines, which were so tall that their tips nearly blocked the sunset. Looking up at the tops of the evergreens, he took in their scent, closing his eyes.

"I promise I'll always love you, Carla. You know that. But I met a woman. We didn't have what you'd call a regular courtship, but I suppose you already know that from where you are." He laughed a little, bittersweet, soft. Wistful.

Then, after listening to the song of the pines around him, he started again. "You really would've liked her. She's lighthearted, down-to-earth, laughs a lot. I'm not sure how she feels about me right now, but I'm hoping…"

The wind picked up, and the branch nearest him nodded above his head.

Adam had never believed in mystic things, but it felt like a positive sign to him. And maybe it was just his imagination, but it seemed a good omen that all the lower tree branches around him had started to resemble open arms.

This was truly the moment.

Moving closer to a tree, he took a deep breath, opened the jewelry box, then spread the ashes in the wind, the pines catching them. He'd never forget. And any woman in his life would understand that.

As twilight folded over the sky, he knew it was time to get out of the dark. Finally time. But first he dug an impromptu hole with a big branch, burying the box, marking its place with a bough.

The sun went down as the wind stopped blowing, leaving everything in peace.

ON MARGOT AND Clint's ranch near Visalia, Leigh was in the midst of twenty women while feeling very much alone.

It was Dani's surprise wedding-planning party, which Margot and Leigh had decided to throw just to bring Dani out of her funk. They were all waiting for Margot to bring her back from the early movie they'd gone to see while Leigh had begged off, claiming that she felt sick.

As the guests, most of them sorority sisters, chatted, Leigh checked around, making sure everyone was comfortable and that they all had notepads for brainstorming for the reception, as well as full wineglasses.

But even with all the laughter, she felt as hollow as a person could get.

Adam hadn't gotten in contact with her, and in spite of everything, there'd been one tiny sparkle of hope in her that he would. Who was she fooling, though? You couldn't make a man fall out of love with his deceased wife, and Leigh didn't even want him to. Carla had obviously been a huge part of who Adam was, and Leigh would never ask anyone to turn his back on that part of his life. It would've been like asking her to forget her sister—the good times, when they would sneak under Hannah's blanket during grade-school nights, using the flashlight to read Judy Blume books together. The times when Hannah would experiment with makeup on Leigh, then wipe it off her face when they heard their parents down the hall. *You don't need makeup anyway,* Hannah would always say. *You're just gonna charm the boys to death, believe me.*

No, Leigh wouldn't have taken such memories from anyone. It was just that she'd been so sure that *she* might be enough to have a place in Adam's life, too. There'd been so much promise there, but now it was over.

A stir in the living room roused her, and Leigh pulled herself out of her funk, rushing toward the window to see if a car had pulled up.

It was Margot's Prius. Leigh told everyone to hunker down as Margot led a blindfolded Dani out of the car and toward the ranch house.

God, the last thing Leigh had wanted to see was a blindfold, but Margot had persuaded her that it was necessary to complete Dani's planning party.

The front door opened, closed, and the next thing

Leigh knew, Margot was standing with Dani at the entrance to the room, pulling off her blindfold.

"Surprise!" everyone yelled.

Amid the laughter, Dani held a hand to her mouth. Her bobbed curly red hair was held back in a short ponytail today, and she was garbed in a new flowered dress that was a little tighter than the ones she used to wear.

After Leigh had left Adam behind, she'd indeed gone to Dani, on a quest to cheer her up from that last phone call while forgetting about her own sorrows. And although Dani had made it her mission to pad Leigh's smarting heart and thighs with enough baked goods to shame Martha Stewart, Leigh had gotten the feeling that Dani was only distracting herself from her own issues and there was something still niggling at her about the upcoming wedding.

"Put the veil on her!" someone yelled.

"Give her the bouquet!"

As Dani stood there, her gaze huge, everyone began to clap and chant.

"Bride-to-be! Bride-to-be!"

Silently, Dani held up a finger, and the volume lowered. "I've really gotta pee, guys. Just a sec."

Everyone thought that was pretty funny as she scooted off. Margot shrugged and announced that they'd had some coffee on the way back from the movie.

While the guests sat back down, Margot found her way to Leigh, who'd taken a seat near the fireplace. No amount of flames could warm her up, though. Not these past few days.

"Brighten up," Margot said, plopping down next to her. She looked svelte in her designer jeans and cashmere sweater. Leigh glanced at the engagement ring on

Margot's finger, and she felt cloudy enough. But she wouldn't be a drag on everyone else.

"I'm a happy partygoer," Leigh said, smiling.

But the excuse didn't wash with Margot. "Just call Adam, would you? You know how to contact Beth, and she can—"

"I can't." Leigh pulled at the sleeve of her tight silk blouse. "He doesn't want to have anything to do with me or he would've stopped me from leaving that day. Besides, he's too..."

"Haunted?" Margot only sighed, having nothing to add. Even a mastermind like her couldn't come up with a way to get around Adam's big emotional obstacles.

They waited for Dani to come back. Waited some more. Finally, it became uncomfortably obvious that something was wrong.

Clint poked his head into the room to crook a finger at his fiancée, and after asking one of their sorority sisters to start brainstorming ideas for a reception that Dani would love, Leigh went with Margot to the kitchen to join Clint.

He leaned against the counter, his golden hair free of the cowboy hat he usually wore, his posture lackadaisical in his typical jeans and Western shirt.

"You looking for Dani?" he asked. At their nods, he motioned toward the back door with his thumb. "She just flew right on out of here. I happened to be walking toward the house from the stables, but she didn't see me."

"What?" Margot asked.

Leigh blew out a breath. "It was the veil and bouquet we wanted her to wear."

Clint interjected. "Just so you know, Riley was planning to come over today. We thought we'd give you all another surprise because he's bringing a keg for a real party. Maybe you two could see what's up with Dani before he gets here?"

"On it." Margot, who wasn't a traditionalist, didn't seem to mind that Riley intended to crash the bridal party. "Which direction did Dani go?"

"Toward the gazebo, I think," Clint said.

The big gazebo, where the wedding ceremony was supposed to take place.

Quickly, Margot planted a kiss on his cheek, then tweaked it. "Thanks. Can you entertain the girls for a bit? I know it's not out of your wheelhouse, you womanizer, you."

"Very funny. Those days are gone and you know it, Hemingway." Just one of many literary nicknames he used for his English major.

Leigh had already opened the door, and they rushed toward the gazebo, hoping Clint was right and that Dani hadn't made it to her car and peeled out of here.

Luckily, the gazebo wasn't all that far, and when Leigh saw Dani sitting inside, bent over, she and Margot slowed down, catching their breath.

"Oh, this is bad," Margot said. "Isn't this bad?"

"I had a feeling that a breakdown wasn't out of the question."

They cut the chatter as they approached, and when Dani heard them, she straightened up, her hand to her chest.

"Can't...breathe...." she said.

"Oh, honey." Margot rushed in, sitting on one side while Leigh took the other.

Even so, they gave her room while trying to comfort her.

Dani's breath did smooth out, but she was still paler than usual. "This is it. Everything's becoming so official. Veils, bouquets, plans upon plans…."

Margot and Leigh exchanged glances.

"Don't worry," Dani assured them. "I'm going to marry Riley. I just don't know when."

She leaned down, elbows on knees, burying her face in her hands. "I'm a disaster, aren't I? The more time I have to think about what I'm getting into, the more time I have to *re*think it. Margot, are you this freaked out about marrying Clint?"

Margot was as blunt as usual. "No."

Dani put her hands to her face again, and Leigh blasted Margot a death look before rubbing Dani's back.

"Just breathe, Dan."

Even as she soothed her friend, she knew all too well what it was like to think that the past was going to consume everything about your present. But it wasn't a parental divorce and a cheating dad that dogged Leigh—it was a man who wouldn't forget *his* past.

"You can't just assume with no hope for a happy future," she said to Dani, thinking of Callum…no, *Adam*… and his continued loyalty to Carla. "You can't give up without even trying."

As Dani turned her head to listen to Leigh, Margot was just as interested.

She asked, "Are you talking about you and Adam?"

"Yeah. And you know what? If I'd had some time to think about it before I turned my back on him, I would've realized that I needed to give him the opportunity to show me that I can still be important to him, even with his struggles."

Leigh thought about that some more as Margot said,

"Just like Riley deserves the chance, too, Dan. He's an honorable guy who's never let you down. You can't go on assuming that he will."

"You've got to make your *own* life with him," Leigh whispered.

Wow, did that sound easy. But couldn't it be? Shouldn't she have given Adam more of an opportunity to let her do just that? And how could she lecture Dani on this if she didn't have the guts to do it herself?

"Make my own life," Dani repeated. "Maybe if I keep saying that, those other crazy thoughts will go away."

Margot nodded. "You can't have a marriage if you don't find some way to banish those fears."

"I know," Dani said. "God, don't I know it...."

A sound from outside the gazebo distracted them, and when Leigh looked up she saw Riley, his dark hair ruffling in the breeze and his mile-long legs eating up the distance, striding toward them. Before any of them could ask what was going on, he barged into the gazebo and headed straight for Dani.

"Clint told me you took off from your own party," he said.

"I—"

Not waiting for her answer, he bent down, scooped her up and hefted her over his shoulder, turning on his heel and walking out of the gazebo.

Dani pushed at his back and yelled, "What're you doing?"

"Something I should've done a long time ago." He kept heading toward the house. "We're not going to wait even another day to get married, Dani."

13

OUTSIDE THE LIL' Big Heart Wedding Chapel on the south end of the Vegas Strip, Leigh tossed rice at Dani and Riley with several other guests who'd made the spontaneous road trip.

The bride and groom had only now just run out of the chapel door and under the white awning with the latticed posts, holding hands, laughing. Dani clutched the lily bouquet that'd come with the quickie wedding package, a small veil covering her short red hair, but she was wearing the same pretty, simple flowered dress she'd started with today.

It'd all come together as rapidly as Riley had wanted it to when he'd shouted his intentions to Clint back at the ranch house while he stuffed Dani into the front seat of his pickup.

"We're heading to Vegas, and whoever wants to come better do it fast!" he'd said before closing his door, then taking off.

Of course, the party guests had dispersed at that point. A few of the wilder sorority sisters had grabbed their purses from inside the house. Then they'd zoomed off after Riley's pickup, yelling, "Marriage or bust, whoo-hoo!" out the window as Clint, Margot and Leigh had watched in shock.

Riley wasn't the reckless type, but he'd clearly had enough of Dani's cold feet.

Then, with a "What the hell," Leigh, Margot and Clint had run into the house, closed it up, grabbed Dani's purse and a few necessities, let the ranch staff know where they were going and zoomed off on the five-hour-plus drive to Vegas. Soon they caught up to the others, thanks to Clint's lead foot. The entire time, Margot and Leigh were in contact with Riley on his Bluetooth as they tried to find a chapel with openings that evening. They'd lucked out with a last-minute cancellation.

Now Dani, who'd gotten into the spirit and kicked off her shoes inside, was a barefoot bride on a red carpet. She stood on her tiptoes to kiss Riley, who was wearing the jeans and Western shirt he'd had on earlier. It didn't look as if she had any misgivings now that she'd jumped headfirst into this. Riley's put-his-foot-down gesture had sure done the job, although Leigh was pretty sure Dani was going to need support as she went along.

As the sorority sisters cheered the married couple, Clint swept Margot into his arms, apparently inspired by this romantic turn of events. Leigh stood apart from them all, watching.

Just as Callum used to watch.

She was happy for Dani and Riley, and for Margot and Clint as well, but she felt lonelier than ever. Why hadn't she cooled down after her confrontation with Adam and given him that chance she'd talked about with Dani today? Had leaving Adam been worth it?

Dani broke off her kiss with Riley, staring up into

his loving gaze. Clint and Margot separated just long enough to toss Riley the extra coats they'd brought, knowing that he and Dani didn't have anything packed.

"Warm her up," Clint said to his friend.

While Riley put the smaller coat over Dani's shoulders, he jerked his chin to Clint. "You don't have to tell me what a honeymoon's all about."

Laughter filled the air around them, the fairy lights on the awning making the night magical. But Leigh merely huddled into her own coat, trying to find warmth.

When Dani turned around and all the other women except Margot gathered to catch the bouquet, Leigh stood toward the back. The flowers sailed right at her, and as that single blip of hope she'd felt earlier started to expand, one of her sorority sisters grabbed the bouquet from in front of Leigh's face.

"Sorry, baby," said Jessica Huntly, with her good-time smile. "Ya snooze, ya lose!"

Well, it wasn't anything Leigh hadn't been telling herself for the past few days.

One of the sisters handed Dani back her shoes, and they all kissed and hugged the newlyweds goodbye. Then the women headed over to a waiting limo, unwilling to waste one more minute of their night in Vegas.

Dani came over to Leigh and Margot while Riley took care of last-minute matters with the chapel staff. "I still say my parents are going to throw a fit because I eloped."

"They saw the ceremony on the webcam," Leigh said. So had Riley's parents, and anyone else who'd been invited to the official wedding next month had access, too.

"Dani." Margot hung her arms over Leigh's and Dani's shoulders. "We'll just turn what should've been your wedding on the ranch into a massive reception. You and Riley can even take your vows again."

Dani smiled, then brought them all into a group hug. "I love you guys, you know. You've stayed with me through thick and thin."

Leigh held them close, the best friends she'd ever had. "What else would you expect? We love you, too."

"Me three," Margot said.

Tears scratched Leigh's throat as they huddled together. One friend married now. One engaged. One…

Well, one so very glad for the other two.

Another white limo—this one included in the wedding package—pulled up. A driver got out to open the door. The plan was for Dani and Riley to climb in and start on the champagne while Margot drove Leigh in her pickup to Caesars Palace, where they'd managed to book a few rooms, and Clint took care of Riley's vehicle. They would all meet up at the hotel before hitting the town.

After Dani got into the limo, Riley prepared to do the same, stopping to playfully waggle his eyebrows at Clint. Then he jauntily waved goodbye to Leigh and Margot before he shut the door.

Dani had already popped out of the open sunroof, though, raising her hands in a sign of triumph. "I'm married!"

And the bright smile on her face didn't lie. She was over the moon, a stronger woman than she'd been a month before, and surprisingly happy about the turn her life had taken. She disappeared back down into the limo, where Riley had no doubt pulled her.

"So what do you think, Shakespeare?" Clint asked Margot, slipping his arm around her waist. "Do you want to move up the honeymoon, too?"

"I'm going to make you wait." But she kissed him anyway, and they both laughed, their lips still brushing each other's.

Giddy. So in love. Leigh sighed.

Now that the bride and groom were behind the darkened limo windows, Leigh dropped her mask, wondering if she'd be able to get through the night without breaking down and crying over her champagne.

A car pulled up on the other side of Dani and Riley's limo, but Leigh barely noticed. "Ready to get going, you two?" she asked the lovebirds.

"Ready," Margot said.

Just then the wedding limo pulled away, revealing the sleek black sports car behind it.

And the man who'd just stepped out of it.

For the longest moment in recorded history, Leigh stared at him, thinking she was dreaming—that all her longing for love had materialized even before she'd gotten herself nice and drunk.

Adam, with his black hair and golden eyes that yearned for her as he just stood there in his flannel shirt and jeans and boots.

He left his car door open and came toward Leigh. "You're here."

Next to her, Margot reached out to grasp Leigh's coat. She and Clint both went still.

"What're you doing?" Leigh asked, numb, still not believing that this was happening.

"It's a long story."

Getting the hint, Clint dragged Margot away, leaving Leigh with Adam in front of the white wedding tunnel, where the fairy lights seemed as if they were from a whole other world.

Adam nodded to Clint as he left—he'd obviously recognized him from his short time in the fraternity—but his attention returned to Leigh full force.

His voice was gritty when he said, "Beth had told me where you went after you left San Diego. And she said you'd be throwing a party for Dani on Margot and Clint's ranch this weekend. So I went there. The ranch hand in charge thought I was supposed to be a part of the festivities or something, so he told me where you all had gone, including which chapel you'd be at if I wanted to attend the wedding. So I drove here as fast as I could."

This *was* Adam, right? The man who'd always hung back from her? But he'd stepped out of hiding and sought her out this time.

"Why'd you come here?" she asked.

"Because I couldn't say what I want to say over the damned phone. I wanted it to be face-to-face."

From Adam straight to Leigh, no go-betweens, no barriers.

Hope was more than a blip now, and it was beeping in her, low and deep. "And what did you want to tell me?"

He looked down, and for a second Leigh thought he'd lost his courage to say what he'd come all these miles to say. But when he glanced back up, she saw the same intensity in his gaze that had been there on the day he'd revealed himself to her.

Was this for real? Somehow she kept thinking that this was just another game. The worst one of all.

"After you were gone," he said, "I couldn't stand it. Not having you there took away all the life around me, and that's when I realized what you'd brought to me. With you, I could laugh again. I could smile and be carefree. There was light when you were around me, and when you left, it left with you."

Her heart felt as if it were bleeding. He'd come all these miles and put her above everything else to be here?

It'd finally happened to her—someone caring, someone wanting to be with her to such an extent that he'd gone ridiculously out of his way for her. But he'd had so many things holding him back, keeping him from truly giving himself to anyone else....

He must've known what she was thinking. "I made my peace with Carla. That's something you did for me, too, Leigh. You showed me it was okay to move on. All you have to do is believe that I'm more than ready now."

"Have you really changed?" Because she couldn't stand if she was wrong, giving everything she had to him and then getting crushed.

"Yes," he said, smiling at her softly. "I have."

It was the first time she'd seen a smile like that from Adam, and her heart reached out, beating for him.

He said, "You're everything I want and need, and I was an absolute mystery to myself until you came along to help me figure things out. Can you believe me?"

She allowed her heart to win, running to him, answering yes with a kiss that could leave no doubts. And she pressed her mouth to his with such passionate pressure that she just about dissolved altogether.

Their first real kiss.

She clung to him, this man who could bring her to intoxicating heights. He explored her in the most desperate of ways, deepening the kiss until she almost fell down.

Whimpering under his mouth, she angled against him, wrapping her arms around his waist, impulsively bringing him closer.

This had to be the kiss of all kisses, with Adam ultimately breaking off to plant more tiny ones on her jaw, her neck, behind her ear. Each of them made delight pop inside of her.

It was only when he paused, his face against her neck, that she opened her eyes and thought, *Callum never kissed me.*

But Callum was in the past. The future was all Adam, who'd come here and put himself on the line for her.

He pulled back slightly, holding her face in his hands, drinking in the sight of her. "Leigh…I've been wanting to do that for so long."

In a whisper, she asked a question she'd put to him before, but it was under very different circumstances now.

"And what's next on the agenda?"

Adam smiled, unmasked, his heart in his gaze.

THEY CHECKED IN to the room Leigh had reserved at Caesars Palace. It had a view of the blue-lit pools, the decor of a Roman getaway and a king-size bed.

That was actually the first thing Adam had noticed upon entering, but he wasn't about to push Leigh into anything they weren't ready for.

Yet when she rushed toward him after closing the door, drawing him into another kiss, he lost all sense of propriety.

His head swirled as he tasted her lips, smelled her strawberry-lotion skin, devoured her while hearing her make small sounds of pleasure under his mouth.

Those sounds drove him on as he sipped at her, and he loosened her hair from its ponytail, digging his hands into all that silk, feeling it glide over his fingers.

When he couldn't catch another breath, he buried his face in her neck. "We could just talk, you know."

"We've got all night to talk." But her agitated tone made him think that she had other things in mind for the night.

Her actions made him think the exact same thing as she all but ripped off her silk blouse, revealing smooth flesh and a demure flower-laced bra.

"Touch me, Adam," she said, and he realized that this would be their first time face-to-face with their clothes off. Callum had been a fantasy, a prelude to a bigger tune, just like the country-noir music that had been playing when Adam had shown her who he truly was. Now it was time for the rest of the piece.

His body assumed the tempo of an upbeat love song as she took him by the hands, resting his knuckles against her mouth, kissing him.

"There was a time," she said against him, "when I didn't know much more about you than your hands and voice. And even though I had no idea who you were, I knew your hands were strong yet gentle at the same time. Just like your words could be."

And those hands were itching to feel her.

He rested his fingertips on her collarbone, tracing her. He wanted to map every inch of the woman he needed in his life so badly that he'd driven all day without a thought to consequence just to be with her, to tell her as soon as he could that she was his light.

Her chest rose and fell as he swept his fingers down over her breasts. Her nipples were already beaded underneath her bra, which hooked in the front. He undid the clasp, watching as her breasts fell free of the cups.

So pink, so pretty.

His blood thudding like a slowly plucked bass, he backed up, toward the bed, sitting on it. She stood before him now, shrugging off her bra.

"My beautiful Leigh," he said, leaning forward, brushing his cheek against her, her nipple skimming him.

He leaned to her other breast, kissing it as her hand threaded in his hair, pulling it a little. She was canting toward him, encouraging him, her long hair unbound and curtaining him.

With heartfelt deliberation, he stroked his tongue from the underside of her breast upward, tasting the salt and musk on her skin. He licked again, this time toward her nipple, just grazing the tip of it.

A gasp told him that he'd hit a mark. She was his just as much as he was hers.

He kept lightly teasing her with his tongue until she grasped his hair harder, letting him know that she was ready for more. So he took her into his mouth, sucking at her, bringing her down closer to him until she had one knee on the bed.

"Adam," she said dreamily. "Adam…"

Coaxing a hand between her thighs, he rubbed her there, through her jeans. Now the rhythm of that bass in him was picking up, strings played with more force, pushing up the tempo of the song in his heart.

"I like hearing you say my name," he whispered, pressing his fingers upward against her clit.

She gasped and looked into his eyes, and the dark green of them swallowed him up.

"Adam," she said almost angrily, because he was circling her now, making her move her hips, teasing her.

He laughed, and she did, too. Then he unbuttoned the

fly of her jeans and shucked them all the way off, along with her boots and socks. She did the same to him, until they were both bare to each other. He pulled her onto his lap so that she straddled him. Over her shoulder, a mirror reflected her gorgeous back and her shapely ass. His hands traveled over her bottom, coming to cup her. Then, parting her thighs more, urging her even closer to him, he watched in that mirror as he slid two fingers up and into her.

While she moaned, he watched as he worked her in and out, making her move up and down. But when she leaned her head back, coming along for the churning ride, the mirror wasn't good enough, and he put his hand behind her head, bringing her face-to-face with him.

Delirious desire was building in her gaze, and that fed him, forced the music in him to go a little faster… *bam-bam-bam,* the bass in his pulse pounding….

He was so hard for her now, his erection echoing the rhythm, that the song was becoming a mess of notes, muddling his mind.

It seemed the most natural thing in the world when he brought her even closer to him, reaching down with his hand to his cock so he could guide it into her as she slid over him.

As he entered her, she made a chest-deep noise, surprised and satisfied at the same time. Her gaze met his, because this was the first time…

The only time he'd fallen for a woman since he'd faded away from life.

But Leigh had brought him back, and she rocked against him, gazing into his eyes the whole time. He didn't look away—couldn't look away—as they moved together in a dance far more intimate than the one they'd shared on the San Diego ranch.

Notes, slamming into him...coming faster, shaping themselves into a song he didn't recognize but, all the same, he swore was familiar. Faster...wilder. The song wasn't stopping, and neither were they as he pulled Leigh down into a soul-searing kiss, taking as much of her as he could get while she strained, labored, arched up with a cry—

She came, and he wasn't too far behind her, in the throes of a blinding whirl of sound and fury.

Stronger, faster, until the sounds somehow turned into something he could see, bright and hot, throbbing, blooming and firing into him—

His orgasm consumed him, taking everything he had as he collapsed back onto the bed, bringing Leigh with him, stretched over his humming body. She pushed back his hair, her skin dewy, watching his face, smiling.

"Adam Morgan," she whispered. "Good to meet you."

He smiled, too, wrapping her in his arms, knowing just who he was for the first time in too long.

Epilogue

"HIDE YOUR EYES," Adam said.

As he led Leigh into the stables of his San Diego ranch, she pressed her hands over her eyes, depending on him to guide her inside the building. Adam had promised her surprises, and they'd never stopped coming during the months they'd been together.

"Stop peeking," he said.

"I'm not." But she was. She decided to obey him, though, squeezing her fingers tighter to show him she could be trusted.

When she heard the nickers of the horses in the barn, she thought that there were more than usual, and she couldn't resist a moment longer, removing her hands just as Adam stood in front of her, putting a stop to her progress.

Adam dressed in the cowboy duds he'd been wearing ever since they'd moved onto this property where they'd had so many good times together. Where they'd finally taken off the blinders and found each other.

"You're making me wait," she said.

He took her face in his hands, smiling down at her.

Her heart zapped around in her chest like a ricocheting bullet.

"Happy four-month anniversary, Leigh," he said, stepping out of the way.

In a stall, a chestnut quarter horse stood, checking her out with big brown eyes.

Leigh let out a squeal. "You didn't!"

"I did." Adam patted the male on the neck, rubbing it. "He goes along with your Bessie Blue. I figured everyone on this place needs some company."

Next door in her own stall, Bessie presented her head, asking Leigh to rub her neck. Leigh went over to her sweetheart, reassuring her thoroughly before heading to the new boy.

"What's his name?" she asked Adam.

"I figured I'd leave that up to you."

"Buddy Blue. It has a nice family ring to it."

"Sounds good to me."

"Thank you so much for this!" She went into her man's arms. Not only had he given her Bessie as a gift right after they'd declared their feelings for each other, he'd also converted his home in Cambria into business offices where Beth was now headquartered.

It was time to let go of the past, he'd told her. Time to start a new life with her and her alone.

Number one, Leigh thought, kissing him until she couldn't breathe anymore. She had no doubt she came first with Adam and always would.

Even when their kiss was done, he swooped Leigh up into his arms. "You happy?"

"I am. But you'd better put me down before you strain yourself."

She was kidding about the few pounds she'd put on

after cooking decadent meals for him every week, but his gaze still adored her every time they were together.

The games hadn't ended with them. Now they were just…safer, Leigh thought. At least as far as their emotions went. They still had their adventures, like the skinny-dipping night in the swimming hole on Clint's ranch after Dani and Riley had taken their vows in front of their families and friends. Or like the toys they played with every weekend after both of them had gotten all their work done and come home to be together again.

But no matter the game, she had no doubt that he would always reveal himself to her, inside and out. He was her Adam, through and through.

"You're light as a feather," he said as he kept lifting her.

She laughed, secure in the fact that he would think she was beautiful even if she gained everything back—which she wouldn't. But still.

She bent down to kiss him again, and they disengaged only when Bessie and Buddy moved closer, nuzzling each other.

"Fast friends," Leigh said.

"More than friends. They've already taken a shine to each other."

"Not more than I've taken a shine to you."

He let her slide down the rest of his body—hard muscles, lean length…promises, promises.

She leaned against him, wrapping her arms around his waist, bringing him in even closer. "I met you here, too, in the stables. The real Adam. Did you ever think…?"

"That I was going to fall head over heels for you?

Yeah. Because I already had. It just took me a while to realize it."

"I think I knew that first night. There was something about you that no one else I'd ever met had."

"Money?"

"No." She squeezed him.

He caught his breath, laughing. "A sense of mystery?"

"Maybe. But there was also a feeling.... Call it women's intuition, but I heard a tenderness in your voice even then."

"Can you hear it now?" He bent to her, whispering against her lips. "I love you, Leigh."

She couldn't miss it. "I love you, too."

As he kissed her, she heard a million whispers in her head and in her body, colliding, then melting together, meant to be.

Meant to become one.

He lifted her to him again with his strong hands, still kissing her until everything blossomed between them into a flare so bright that she forgot all of the darkness that'd been there before.

Into the light, she thought as he kept kissing her.

And into a beautiful future.

* * * * *

Have Your Say

You've just finished your book.
So what did you think?

We'd love to hear your thoughts on our 'Have your say' online panel
www.millsandboon.co.uk/haveyoursay

- 🌹 Easy to use
- 🌹 Short questionnaire
- 🌹 Chance to win Mills & Boon® goodies

*Visit us
Online*

Tell us what you thought of this book now at
www.millsandboon.co.uk/haveyoursay

YOUR_SAY